# Insight's Most
# UNFORGETTABLE
# STORIES

### Compiled by
### Christopher Blake

REVIEW AND HERALD® PUBLISHING ASSOCIATION
HAGERSTOWN, MD 21740

This book was
Designed by Bill Kirstein
Typeset:10.5/12 Sabon

Texts credited to NIV are from the *Holy Bible, New International Version.* Copyright © 1973, 1978, International Bible Society. Used by permission of Zondervan Bible Publishers.

Bible texts credited to RSV are from the Revised Standard Version of the Bible, copyrighted 1946, 1952 © 1971, 1973.

Bible texts credited to TEV are from the *Good News Bible*—Old Testament: Copyright © American Bible Society 1976; New Testament: Copyright © American Bible Society 1966, 1971, 1976.

The story title "Gooley Flies Again" originally appeared in *I Saw Gooley Fly,* by Joseph Bayly. Copyright © 1968 by Fleming H. Revell Company, Old Tappan, N.J. Used by permission.

PRINTED IN U.S.A.

97 96 95          10 9 8 7 6 5 4 3

**R&H Cataloging Service**
Insight
    Insight's most unforgettable stories.
Compiled by Christopher Blake.

    1. Religious literature—Collected works.
2. Christian literature—Collected works.
I. Blake, Christopher, compiler. II. Title.

808.803

ISBN 0-8280-0557-5

# Contents

## CHRISTMAS

## FAITH

# Foreword

Even if you haven't heard of *Insight*, the Christian youth magazine that began in 1970, you are going to like this collection of stories. In fact we predict you'll find yourself marking your favorites on the contents page, and then eagerly reading them again and sharing them with friends.

These short stories may be used for speeches, skits, devotions, or simply for personal enjoyment. And they'll be unforgettable to readers for various reasons, whether for leaving a tear in the eye, an *ahhh* on the lips, or the residue of what Robert Frost meant when he wrote, "Writing helps us to remember things we never knew we knew."

From the past 20 years we've gleaned 60 wonderful stories—and we had plenty left over. If we didn't include a favorite of yours, let us know; we're planning to produce another volume in the future.

Acknowledgments should go to the *Insight* editors (for longtime *Insight* readers this list will bring back memories): Don Yost (1970-71); Roland Hegstad (1971-72); Mike Jones (1972-75); Donald John (1975-81); Dan Fahrbach (1982-1985); and Christopher Blake (1986-present).

In addition we appreciate the work of the associate and assistant editors, the backbone of any magazine: Pat Horning Benton (1970-73); Chuck Scriven (1970-73); Judy Rittenhouse (1973-74); Ken McFarland (1974-75); Karen Spruill (1975-77); Marquita Halstead (1977-1981); Deborah Anfenson-Vance (1982-84); Kris Coffin Stevenson (1984-86); and Lori Tripp Peckham (1986-present).

And because it doesn't go without saying, this book would not be in your hands without the efforts of the many editorial secretaries, student interns, and editorial assistants who helped to bring stories to print. In particular I'm grateful to Barbara Wells, our editorial secretary, for her hours of work on the project, and to assistant editor Lori Peckham for her invaluable aid in organizing. A big thank you is also extended to Nettie Anderson, Clara Burtnett, Richard Coffen, and Penny Estes Wheeler of the Review and Herald® Publishing Association.

Moreover, for months of enduring stacks of bound *Insight* volumes all around our house, my ardent love and gratitude go to my wife, Yolanda, and to our sons, Nathan and Geoffrey.

Finally and best, thank You to the gracious God of the universe, the creator of creativity, who loves us all.

*Christopher Blake*

# FAMILY

**What one object would you pick as a symbol for the closest link in human relations? Would it be a brooch? A fiddle? A note? A lantern?**

**Not likely. But those are what four writers in our opening section chose. You'll also find the shared agonies of "Chomba" and "Secret Likeness," the amazing patience of "Going Home," the final, startling recognition of "He's My Brother" and "My Father's Daughter."**

**Only one word in our language can fit them all. Family.**

◆ ◆ ◆

# Wear It on the Inside

## *Lori Lynn Pettibone*

STANDING in the bedroom doorway, I watch as she searches through her closet. A large blue bathrobe wraps snugly around her ample figure, and her freshly washed hair is wound up in curlers.

Unaware of my presence, she hums a tune. It seems like ages since I've seen her so happy. But then again, it's been ages since she's had any reason to be happy.

Tonight she's preparing to go on her first date—at least her first date since Daddy left. She pulls out a dress from the closet. Turning to look in the mirror, she glances my way.

"What do you think?" she asks.

I nod my head, "It's beautiful."

I remember my first date three years ago. How Daddy had kept quiet all evening, afraid he'd say something wrong. How Katrina had more than made up for his silence by chanting continuously, "Someone has a boyfriend! Someone has a boyfriend!" How Mama had given me the brooch.

"I want you to have this," she had said as she handed it to me.

"My mother gave it to me when I went on my first date." She had looked at it and chuckled. "Of course, I thought it was ugly. But if you wear it on the inside of your pocket, no one will ever know you have it on." And then she had hugged me.

*Was that the last time she hugged me?* I wonder as I watch her put on her makeup. I can't remember.

It had been around then that the trouble started between her and Daddy, and he had walked out, taking Katrina with him.

It had also been around then that I started coming in after curfew and missing meals.

"You're never home anymore," she mentioned one Saturday evening as I was preparing to go out.

I had snapped at her. I don't remember exactly what I said; I only remember the hurt that escaped from her eyes as she turned and slowly left my room. My guilt and my pride wouldn't allow me to apologize.

*How she must have hurt,* I think as I remember how I began to yell more and more, even going as far as telling her that I hated her.

And not once had she yelled back, not once had she given me the treatment that I knew I deserved. Had that been why I hated her? Because she had continued to love me although I had not treated her right?

I watch as she peers into the mirror, brushing on mascara, her hand trembling slightly. And for the first time I see past the mask of motherhood into her heart, where she has always been a little girl, afraid and lonely, yet hopeful. Hopeful that everything would be all right again—the way it would have been if Daddy had never left.

I had once been hopeful, also. But I had long since lost that hope. I had given up on ever being happy again. Yet now as I watch my mother, I know that somewhere deep inside me that hope still remains, waiting only to be proved.

Silently I watch as Mother rummages through a drawer. Then turning to me, she asks, "Do you have my hand mirror in your room?"

"Oh, yeah," I say quickly as I jump up to get it for her. Crossing my cluttered room, I notice the brooch sitting on my windowsill. Picking it up, I turn and carry it gingerly to my mother's room.

"Mother," I say, surprised at the softness of my voice, "I want you to have this." I look down at my hands nervously before continuing. "I know you think it's ugly, but if you wear it on the inside of your pocket . . ."

I feel the soft touch of her hand on mine as she takes it and pins it on the front of her dress.

"It's the most beautiful thing I've ever seen," she says. And as a tear falls from the corner of her eye, she hugs me.

♦ ♦ ♦

# Chomba

## *Arthur A. Milward*

WHEN he asked me, just as I was about to hear him say his bedtime prayer: "Daddy, is Chomba a Christian?" I didn't know how to answer him.

He was 3 years old, and Chomba was his favorite among all the African staff at the East African boarding school. Oh yes, he liked old Isaac, the cook, and Isaac watched over him and cared for him as well as any nursemaid. He liked to watch Nzorka, the gardener, and would follow him around as he went about his work (although he was a little bit afraid of him). But it was Chomba, the Kikuyu houseboy, to whom he had grown the closest.

Perhaps it was because Chomba was the youngest of all the Kikuyu tribesmen who were part of the school family. Or perhaps it was because of Chomba's ready smile and never-failing cheerfulness. In fact, the young houseboy's readiness to "go the second mile" without even being asked had endeared him to us all. Whatever the reason, whenever 3-year-old Adrian (Ady for short) was not immediately in evidence and a search was organized to determine his whereabouts (which took place, on the average, six or seven times a day), the inevitable suggestion was: "Go see what Chomba's doing. Ady's probably with him." And nine times out of ten he was.

To return to the original question concerning Chomba's qualifications for inclusion with us Christians, the problem was a bit more complex than it appeared on the surface. For instance, there was the matter of his two wives. A problem for a Solomon, to be sure.

It had become necessary to recruit from outside the Christian community if our mission school was to remain operative. Consequently, our domestic staff was comprised wholly of non-Christian Kikuyu tribesmen. This, we realized, was less than ideal. But they were to a man, willing, cheerful, and industrious, and were therefore pearls of great price, not to be lightly relinquished.

Chomba and I discussed the situation as soon as I was aware that he had moved into his little room in the servants' quarters with his two attractive young wives and tiny baby son.

"Look here, Chomba," I told him, "you must realize that you cannot have two wives here. I recognize that it is tribal custom and perfectly legitimate within your society, but it is contrary to Christian belief and practice."

"But, Bwana," Chomba objected, apologetically, "they are *both* my wives. I married them both in good faith. I can't just throw one out. What would she do? Where would she go?" A couple of good questions if ever there were any.

Finally, we agreed on a compromise. Chomba was to maintain one wife at a time in his quarters at the school. He was to send the other one back to his home in his village in the Highlands. Then if they wanted to "trade off" at intervals, that would be all right with me.

I don't believe anyone other than Chomba and I was aware that the smiling young face hovering over the cooking fire outside Chomba's room in the evening did not always belong to the same young woman. To most, an African was an African, and a servant's wife was not the sort of individual to merit much attention.

Adrian knew though. He used to visit Chomba in his little room and play with the baby, and he quickly learned the names of the folks who lived in the servants' quarters—and their faces.

"Chomba's other mummy came today, Daddy," he informed me. "She's nice."

It was Chomba who first drew our attention to the fact that Ady was not looking well. The little boy had been paler than usual for some days. His cheeks had lost some of their rosiness, and his boundless store of energy seemed strangely diminished. "The toto needs some *dawa* (medicine), Bwana," he suggested, somewhat diffidently. After a little close observation, we were inclined to agree.

The doctor—a skilled and understanding pediatrician—asked a lot of questions, conducted a thorough examination, and scheduled blood and bone-marrow tests. We took Ady home.

The results of the tests were to be ready Friday afternoon. School was out for the day, and I sat in the empty classroom, staring blankly at the half-cleaned chalkboard and trying to control the trembling of my hands. I had wept some, had prayed a lot, and I was deathly afraid.

While in college I had worked as an aide in a big general hospital in England, and the nature of the tests being performed told my mind what my heart refused to believe. I had cared for leukemia patients on a number of occasions.

The doctor came to the house to deliver the results of the tests personally. We did our best to spare each other, but the tears would not be held back.

In a tightly knit little community such as ours, news—good or bad—travels fast. Chomba sought me out in the empty classroom later that evening. I heard his soft-voiced *"Hodi!"* ("Is anyone there?") behind me, but I did not turn my head. He walked up to where I sat in the shadows, his bare feet making no sound on the wooden floor. He stood silent behind my chair for several moments. When he spoke I could tell by his voice that there were tears in his eyes. He put his hand on my shoulder and spoke in Swahili:

"Oh, Bwana," he said, his voice husky with grief. "Our son must die." He began to weep quietly.

It was some months—months that seemed like years—and many miles later that I realized what it was that Chomba had said. *"Our* son . . ." he had said. "Our son must die."

I thought of that conference in heaven millenniums ago and untold miles distant, when the provision had been made that ensured that those who went to sleep in Jesus would rise again. I thought of the love of the heavenly family that had decided—for love of me—that another Son must die. I marveled—and was humbled by the wonder of it all.

If my little son were here now and if he were to ask me again whether Chomba was a Christian, I think I would know how to reply.

◆ ◆ ◆

# When Tulips Die in the Spring

### Ruth Garren

O NLY 9:00 in the morning, and already it was hot. Jenny looked out of her bedroom window. The fields and trees around the house had gone from spring-green to the deeper green of summer in one rainless week.

Her grandfather, whom everyone called Papa John, was working in the garden. She could hear the *tick tick* of his hoe against the dry earth and a few birds chirping.

Last week Jenny had gotten out of school for the summer. Already she knew it was going to be long.

She turned from the window to her dresser, which was covered with trophies: six years of Presidential Fitness awards; a handful of ribbons from Field Day events at school; seven firsts, three seconds, and one grand prize trophy for fiddling in Mountain Youth festivals.

She picked up the newspaper clipping from the Benton *Beacon*, sealed in plastic to keep it from yellowing. Jenny was 5 years old in the photograph, and her great-grandfather, whom she'd always called Grandpa, was 75. The photographer had caught the two of them, dappled in sunlight, through the leaves of a huge oak tree, holding their fiddles and smiling into each other's faces.

The paper read: "Five-year-old Jenny Burrows is a fifth-generation fiddler. Her great-grandfather Clive Sprague, of Benton, and his brother Gus, of Hiwassee, were taught by their father when they were about Jenny's age. Clive, in turn, taught his daughter Helen (now deceased) and his grandson Philip, Jenny's father, who died in Vietnam. 'Jenny's got real talent,' Mr. Sprague comments. 'You've either got it or you don't, and Jenny's got more of it than any young'un I've ever taught—in or out of the family.' Jenny's mother plays the mandolin. Other family members play the bass fiddle, guitars, and banjos. The family group entertains regularly in the Polk County area. Look for them on Old Timers' Day at Big Ridge Park at the same spot under the big oak where family members have gathered a crowd on Old Timers' Day for 70 years."

Jenny studied the photograph. Grandpa's face was criss-crossed with lines. Now the lines had turned to furrows, giving his face character and making him a natural subject for photographers who showed up at every Old Timers' Day.

Jenny set the clipping back on the dresser. *Well, they're in for a surprise this year,* she thought, *because Jenny Burrows, award-winning fiddler, will not be fiddling on Old Timers' Day. She's had enough.* She tied her hair back with a ribbon to lift it from her neck.

Jenny went outside. Her mother was digging holes in the dirt and planting flowers. A drop of sweat balanced on the tip of her nose. Streaks of dirt showed where she had wiped her forehead.

"You look like you've been out here a while," Jenny said.

"A couple of hours."

"And you're going to get one of those redneck tans again, Mom. Just like last year."

"Well, Jenny, the only way to avoid that is to work outside in my bathing suit, and I don't believe I'll be doing that."

Again this spring Mom was mixing petunias and impatiens, snapdragons and begonias, without much thought for color or design.

"Mom," Jenny asked her, not for the first time, "why don't you do all pink things, or all pink and white? This is going to look like a crazy quilt."

"Well, honey, it's the way I like it."

Jenny knew she would say that.

"Mom, I want to talk to you about something."

"Go right ahead."

"I don't want to play for Old Timers' Day Sunday."

"Why not?"

"Because I don't play the fiddle anymore."

"Since when?"

"Since now. I'm beginning to get good on the violin, and I don't want to get myself mixed up."

"What does your teacher say about that?"

"Nothing. He doesn't know I play the fiddle."

"You mean to tell me you've been taking lessons from him for two years and you didn't tell him?"

"No."

"And he's never caught on?"

"No."

"He never thought you were a bit gifted for a beginner?"

"He said I had good tone for a beginner, but I just said thank you and let him teach me technique and everything else, just like I'd never held a bow or a violin before."

"Well, Jenny Burrows," the spade was furiously stabbing the earth, "that is deceitful. That is right next door to an outright lie. Do you think your grandmother would have done that, or your father?"

"I don't know, and I don't care. Fiddling is a hokey thing to do, anyway."

"Hokey? Where did you get that idea? You are going to break your great-grandfather's heart, young lady, and your uncle Gus's, too."

"They'll get over it."

"They're in their 80s. They may not have another Old Timers' Day."

"You're trying to lay guilt on me, Mom. I hate it when you do that. Grandpa and Uncle Gus might as well get used to playing without me. Besides, there's Uncle Gus's family."

"But they've never been as good as you are, and they never will be. And you know it." Mom paused a minute and stood up to confront Jenny at eye level. "You know you can't put your 'hokey' mountain traditions behind you any more than you can deny the fact that you're a fourth-generation Christian."

"Well, the jury is still out on that one."

"Jenny Burrows!" her mother said, shocked.

"What are those ugly things there?" Jenny asked, trying to change a subject she wished she'd never started.

"Those are the last of the tulips."

"Why don't you dig them out?"

"Because it's not time yet. They have to die down completely; then you can just pull the stems out of the ground. I figure I'll put these impatiens there, and pretty soon they'll be big enough so you won't even notice the tulips."

"I'd pull them out."

"I know you would."


Old Timers' Day dawned bright and clear, the kind of weather Jenny used to pray for in the old days. In the kitchen her mom was packing sandwiches and potato salad into the cooler. Mom's mandolin and Jenny's fiddle stood at the back door, ready to be carried to Papa John's van.

"My fiddle's there," Jenny pointed out. "I told you not to pack it."

"It's Papa's van, Jenny, and he'll take it if he wants to."

"Well, do what you want, but you're just taking up space for nothing."

The scene at Big Ridge Park was as noisy, colorful, and confusing as past summers. Some groups were already playing music. Others were standing around talking. People who had come to listen waited with their lawn chairs to see which groups might be worthy of their sitting-down attention.

Grandpa began tuning up. Papa John, who said he'd married his wife, Helen, to get music genes into his family, not because he had any talent to bring to hers, sat in a chair in the shade. He and Helen had had only one child, Philip. Philip and Madge had had only Jenny, and only Jenny was left.

The music began. Grandpa led with a slow, gentle ballad. Jenny noticed that his fingers were stiff and his tone no longer as warm or rich as she remembered it. Still, he was one of the best fiddlers around.

Then someone asked for "Foggy Mountain Breakdown," a fast-clogging number. Grandpa started out playing first fiddle, but his fingers faltered. He nodded toward Gus's son Axel. Axel took over, fumbling a little in the beginning, but not doing too badly. Still, Jenny could see the frustration on Grandpa's face. He was used to being the best.

Jenny remembered how in the old days, when she was just learning, Grandpa's expertise had covered for her immature playing. Could she do any less for him?

She went to the van and got her fiddle. She tuned it as she walked back, holding the instrument, made by Grandpa himself, gently under her chin. She slid in at the edge of the group and began playing second fiddle with Grandpa, her bowing sure and strong, her tone as mellow as his had been in his best years.

He nodded to her, and she took the lead. Her fingers had become stronger and more flexible from violin lessons and typing classes. The music filtered up among the leaves of the oak tree and wafted off toward the mountains that made up Big Ridge. People set their lawn chairs down to relax and listen and watch.

Jenny was taking over for her great-grandfather, covering his weak tones with her strong ones as he had once done for her. Yes, it was right *not* to pull out the tulips—her roots. As the cameras clicked, she again smiled up into Grandpa's furrowed face.

◆ ◆ ◆

# He's My Brother

### *Danny Kim*

IT wasn't until after my parents divorced that I was "blessed" with another brother. And this brother wasn't an innocent little bundle of joy, an infant from my mother's womb.

This brother was a 9-year-old brat who was the product of a strange woman and a previous spouse of hers. A strange woman who was now my father's betrothed.

I was 15 at the time. And I had another brother, a *real* brother. His name was Larry, and he was 13.

FAMILY

Together, our combined age was 28. That meant we were like adults. That meant we shouldn't have to put up with a 9-year-old brat named Chris, a stranger and our brother.

I tried to get along with him. Really, I tried. But I couldn't. He turned out to be a real pest, a 9-year-old thorn in my side.

One time I was playing with a Transformer and Chris decided that he wanted to play with it too. He asked me if he could have it. I told him to go away. But he kept asking, again and again. Why was he so persistent? Couldn't he see that I was busy? He could play with the Transformer later. It *was* his; but right now I was playing with it.

Chris finally grew impatient, and he took the Transformer out of my hands. That did it.

"Give it back, Chris!" I shouted as I leaped to my feet.

"You've been playing with it long enough!" he said, backing away.

He had been a thorn long enough; it was time to pluck him out. I bolted toward him. He turned to run, but my hand was twisted in the tail of his shirt. I had him.

I wrenched the toy from his fingers and wrestled him up against the wall. I grasped the front of his shirt and lifted him up off the ground. With tears burning in my eyes, I screamed: "Chris! Why can't you just leave me alone?"

He stared down at me, lips quivering, face flushed. He was speechless.

I let go of him, and he dropped to the floor. I went back to playing with the Transformer. He didn't bother me again the rest of that evening.

Larry didn't get along with Chris either. They would get into fights, but Larry wasn't much bigger than Chris, so he couldn't nail Chris up against the wall like I could.

I always took Larry's side when he and Chris got into a fight. It's funny how Larry and I would fight like dogs when we were alone, but whenever Chris was around, Larry and I got along perfectly. The thing was this: Chris was a stranger to us, and he didn't know his place.

Every once in a while my conscience would remind me of the words Jesus had said, like "Love your brother." I could do that. Or "Love your enemy." I could do that, too. But Chris was my brother *and* my enemy! That was just too tough for me.

Of course, there were times when we didn't fight. There were some days when we even got along just fine.

I remember one time when my dad and his wife took us to an arcade. That was great! All three of us were video game freaks.

When we arrived, Dad gave us all a handful of quarters, and we galloped to the machines, grinning like Cheshire cats. We even gave each other quarters when we ran out. Or one of us would ask Dad for more and then give some to the other two. We even played doubles with each other. We were completely peaceful when we were at odds with the glowing enemies of the microchip.

But when we got home, things changed. Larry and I got into another argument with Chris.

It always happened that way—no matter how good the day had been. Chris was our stepbrother, and he was invading our home territory.

One time we all came home from a reasonably pleasant day out. It was evening, and we were all joking around on the walkway. Then after my dad and his wife walked into the house, Chris tripped me. I don't know how he did it, but I suddenly found myself sucking mud.

Chris laughed.

"You're gonna get it, Chris!" I threatened.

"Don't!" he pleaded, suddenly not laughing anymore. "I—I—I didn't mean it!"

"Come here!" I yelled.

He ran in the opposite direction.

I took off after him, and Larry followed. I chased him across the street and onto the neighbor's freshly watered lawn.

"I'm gonna get you, Chris!" I roared.

I closed on him. I knew he was getting tired. I could see him in the cold air, puffing out every breath.

I tackled him to the moist ground, wrestled him onto his slimy back. Tears filled his eyes.

"My back's getting all wet!" he wailed.

I glared at him. "Ha!"

"I'm sorry!" he screamed as he covered his face with his hands.

"Too late," I said.

I pinned his arms under my knees. He squirmed like a little worm on the grass.

Larry stood there and laughed.

"Larry!" huffed Chris. "Larry, tell him to stop it!"

Larry shrugged. "You shouldn't have tripped him, Chris."

Chris quit struggling, gave up, continued panting.

"When we get back to the house," I said, "you're gonna tell Dad that we were running around and you tripped and fell."

"I won't!" cried Chris.

I looked up at Larry.

"Did you see what I saw, Lar?"

"Sure did," he said. "We were just running around and Chris just tripped and fell."

"I did not!" clenched Chris as he arched his back, heaved once, and fell limp again.

I started slapping his face. "Chris?" I growled.

He whimpered, had a scrunched expression on his face.

"Chris?" I repeated. I lifted his shirt and exposed his abdomen. "I'm gonna give you a pink belly if you don't give in." I began hitting his stomach, began slapping capillaries open around his belly button.

He sputtered and cried. "OK! OK!"

"OK *what?*" I demanded.

"I'll tell him that I tripped!" he surrendered.

That was all I needed. I dug my fingers into the moist, soft ground and shoved a fistful of mud and grass onto his face, up his nose, down his mouth. I got up off of him. He slowly got up, rubbed the back of his hand across his face, spat onto the ground, and looked at me with heated eyes.

The three of us walked back to the house. Chris walked slightly ahead. He went straight into his room and locked the door. Dad never did ask what happened.

In time my dad divorced this wife, and we were granted the privilege of the absence of Chris. I haven't seen him since.

I was talking to my friend Joe about this the other day—about the hassles of having a stepbrother. Stepbrothers are brats, pests. They cause only grief. Who needs them?

You know what Joe told me? He told me that Chris wasn't my stepbrother.

He said that I was Chris's stepbrother.

◆ ◆ ◆

# Going Home

## Paula Campbell

HER gray eyes could be hard and unforgiving one moment, and in the next instant fade into a vacant stare. She laughed often. When she laughed, the whole room brightened. It was a deep laugh, coming from her heart. And I knew when I heard it that at one time her now-faded smile could have made angels sing.

In an odd, distracted way she'd sit for hours and stare at what appeared to be nothing, a half smile tugging at the corners of her lips. She spoke little, and when she did, I couldn't always understand. Especially at 10 years of age.

Every day Grandma was "going home." She'd get up from her rocking chair by the window and shuffle toward the door. She placed an open hand lightly on the furniture as she walked by, as if she were dusting the table tops.

"Where are you going, Mama?" my mother would call.

"Going home," Grandma would reply in a shaky voice. "I need to go home. Jerry needs me, and Mama will wonder where I am. It's getting late, you know."

"Well, where do you live?" Mama was trying to divert Grandma's attention—or to settle her down somehow. "I'll walk with you."

"Just over that little hill." My gaze followed my grandmother's outstretched arm toward the cornfield. We lived on a farm then. Grandma's farm. The farm where she had worked canning vegetables for the winter. The home where her five children, including my mother, were born and raised. The home in which she had spent 50 years of her life, feeding hoboes, buying war bonds, watching freight trains clack by to places unknown. Grandpa had liked living by the railroad. He was an engineer, and wore the blue-and-white-striped railroadman's cap. He was dead now. And Grandma wanted to go home.

Grandma and Mama would walk down the dirt road,

Mama's arm linked through the crook of Grandma's elbow, past the barns, the chicken coop, the grapevines. Intently, Grandma would peer around every tree and corner—to find home.

And they'd talk as they walked, the two of them. I don't know what about. I never went with them on their little excursions. Grandma scared me when she got like that. I didn't understand her. Or why she wanted to go "home." But I imagine they talked of flowers and birds, whippoorwills especially, and Jerry, and home.

After what seemed like hours of walking, they'd end up right back on the back porch. The boards creaked and their shoes clattered on the wood—Mama's steps firm and steady, and Grandma's shuffle soft and gentle as a curtain brushing against a windowsill.

"It's getting late, and I'm sure your mama wouldn't want you traveling home at dusk. Why don't you just spend the night here with us?"

"But I've got to get home." Grandma's voice sounded anxious, and she'd start to shuffle off the porch.

"Where is it, then? I'll walk with you." Mama's voice was calm.

Tears welled up in Grandma's eyes and she sobbed, "I don't know where it is, I've been looking, and I can't find it. . . ." Her words trailed off.

"Spend the night with me," Mama coaxed. "Maybe in the morning things will look different."

Grandma looked for home for five years. In 1974 she was 9, then 7. Strength had left her, and although she still wanted home she couldn't get out of her chair to find it. She'd scoot herself to the edge, then fall to her knees. Mama would rush over, pick her up, and put her back, placing an afghan gently over her lap.

A scowl would wrinkle Grandma's face, and through pursed lips she'd pout, "I'm gonna bop you one." Her hand, creamy white with every vein evident, would flail at the air, her wedding band burden almost too heavy for her to lift.

"Go ahead," Mama would tease. And she'd pretend to be a boxer, fists clenched, punching the air.

Then Grandma's anger would melt into laughter. They'd laugh, mother and daughter, until Grandma forgot. Usually that wasn't very long. She forgot often.

I watched Grandma turn 3. Then, no more laughter, no more going home. She lay in bed and cooed and babbled.

The day before Thanksgiving, Grandma died. She had fallen asleep and forgotten to wake up. Mama was with her then, too. And I heard her whisper as she kissed Grandma's cheek, "Not long now, Mama, and you'll be home."

◆ ◆ ◆

# My Father's Daughter

## *Deanna Davis*

I TRUDGED past the dreary hotels. In their lobbies aged, forgotten men and women sat, like characters in the last scene of a play who have said all their lines and now must wait, watching the others until the curtain falls. A church bell far in the distance struck 3:00. I had called him at noon to tell him I was on my way, and he knew it was only a 45-minute bus ride from my house to his.

I lingered awhile outside the open door of the Acropolis Tavern and peered through the cloud of smoke at the entryway into the darkness beyond. Perhaps he had tired of waiting for me and had come to have a drink or two.

"Hey, baby, come on in. I'll buy you a drink," called a hopeful from the bar. My feet found new speed, and I hurried down the sidewalk.

This was West Burnside Street, Portland's skid row. Often I had ridden down this street with fellow Christians. Often they had chanted a warning chorus of "Lock your doors! Roll up your windows!" And always I had wondered what those friends would have thought had they known my father lived here.

My parents had divorced shortly before I was born. For much of my life "Mac," as everyone called him, had refused to acknowledge me as his child. Only after my older sister died had he seemed interested in claiming me as his daughter. He had never paid for my support, never had been there when I needed him, never had been a father to me.

I turned the corner at his building and prayed that he'd be sober.

He saw me almost as soon as I saw him. A wide smile filled his face. He stood at his third-floor window and waved vigorously down at me. In that moment he did not seem to be an alcoholic, a convicted felon, or any of the other things I knew he was. Simply a father who had waited more than two hours by his window, watching for his daughter.

The old metal grate on the elevator squealed as I pulled it shut. I pushed the button for the third floor. Then inch by squeaking inch, I was transported upward.

The narrow unlit hallway gave the impression of night. My father's door was standing open, spilling an oval of light onto the threadbare hall carpet. His door was always open. No one passed it without receiving his greeting, not even those who had no greeting to return.

"Hi, honey. How's my girl?"

"Hi, Daddy." My father's once strong arms encircled me. His whiskers brushed my cheek as my arms slipped around his tattered T-shirt. The air close to his body reeked of cigarette smoke, cheap wine, and sweat.

He turned off the TV. "You're looking good. Lost a little weight, haven't you?"

"Oh, a couple of pounds, maybe." I sat beside him on the dirty old couch and looked around at the room that was his home. A large lamp lay disassembled on the table.

"Did you get a new lamp?" I asked.

"No, that belongs to Ralph down the hall. I'm putting a new switch on it for him."

"Oh."

"How long can you stay?"

"Well . . . I'm running a little late. I probably should leave about 6:30. We're having a meeting at the church."

"You'll need something to eat first. I've got some hamburger I can fry up. You can make yourself a sandwich. Want something to drink? I've got root beer." He opened the refrigerator door, revealing three bottles—catsup, root beer, and wine—and one small package wrapped in butcher paper. There was nothing else.

"Sounds good, thanks." He always forgot that I was a vegetarian. I didn't remind him.

His arthritic hands fumbled with the twist-off cap on the pop bottle. He poured me a glass of root beer, taking none for himself. We sat and chatted briefly about my job, the weather, sports, and news.

"Excuse me."

It was a familiar cue. My eyes did not follow him as he turned again toward the refrigerator. Instead, I became politely preoccupied with the path of a large cockroach on the opposite wall.

I heard the refrigerator door open, his hurried swallowing, the tinkle of metal and glass as he placed the wine bottle back on the shelf. The refrigerator door closed.

Daddy and I continued our conversation as though there had been no interruption. I never preached to my dad. I'd given up on converting him. He had been an alcoholic for more than 50 years.

"Wish you could stay longer. But I don't want to interfere with your religion. I'm proud of you, you're a lot like my mother was. I don't belong to any church, but I believe in God. 'Do unto others as you would have them do unto you.' That's my religion." We heard a noise in the hallway.

"Here comes Jake. Hey, Jake, come here. I want you to meet my daughter."

"Hi, Mac!" Jake maneuvered his wheelchair through the door.

"Jake, this is my daughter, Deanna. She works for U.S. National Bank."

"Nice to meet you. Your dad talks about you all the time. You've got a pretty daughter, Mac."

"I think so. And she's a good girl, too." I blushed as the two men beamed at me.

"Say, Mac, could you pick me up a carton of Winstons next time you're out?" Jake asked.

"You know I could."

Jake thumbed through his wallet and produced a ten-dollar bill. "Your dad's my legs," he said, smiling. "And not just mine—he runs errands for lots of folks in this building." My father folded the money and slipped it carefully into his back pocket.

"Well, Mac, I'll be going so you and your daughter can visit."

He turned his wheelchair around and moved back into the hall.

"I'll have those cigarettes for you later tonight," my father called after him.

"You want your sandwich now?" he asked me.

"Sure."

Daddy plugged in the electric skillet I had given him for Christmas two years before. Leftover grease spattered and spit as the hamburger fell into the pan. I wondered how long it had been since the pan had been cleaned.

"There's somebody else I want you to meet."

"Oh, really, who?" I asked.

"Her name is Joanne. She's one of the nicer women in this place. She just had her third brain surgery and is paralyzed on one side. She's really discouraged." He flipped the hamburger patties over and flattened them with his spatula. "I've been checking on her every day to see how she's doing. Day before yesterday I walked into her apartment and found her lying on a bed soaked with blood. She'd fallen out of bed and cut a big gash in her head. Instead of calling for help, she just dragged herself back into bed and decided to bleed to death."

"That's awful."

"I poured styptic powder into the cut and taped a bandage over it. Then I called her doctor. Now she's really mad at me 'cause I wouldn't let her die. I'd like you to meet her. You're good with words. Maybe you can say something to cheer her up."

I picked a small spot of blue mold out of the piece of bread I was buttering. "Sure, I'll meet her."

*Great,* I thought, as I carefully guided my knife through the butter to avoid picking up any of the cigarette ashes that lay on the bottom of the butter dish. *What am I supposed to say to a woman I've never met before who wants to die? "God loves you and has a wonderful plan for your life?"* That just didn't seem to cut it.

My father rapped once on her door and let himself in.

"It's Mac," he called out.

"Go away, Mac," Joanne shouted from the bedroom. "Leave me alone." A storm of profanity added weight to her expressed desire. My dad smiled.

"I've got somebody I want you to meet."

"I don't want to meet anybody. Go away!"

"Perhaps we ought to leave," I suggested. My father smiled again.

"Hope you're decent, 'cause we're coming in." I sheepishly followed my father to Joanne's bedside.

Joanne appeared to be about 60. Her head had been shaved for surgery, and her hair was now only about an inch long. The side of her face that was paralyzed contained a large running sore that she picked at with her good hand. My father's makeshift bandage covered half her head. She smelled horrible.

"Why didn't you let me die?" Her voice was full of hate. "I don't want to live anymore."

"Sure you do," Daddy replied matter-of-factly. "I'd like you to meet my daughter, Deanna."

Joanne's face communicated a big "So what?" She swore.

"Lord, help me," I prayed. There was a pocket Bible in my purse. Perhaps I could read the twenty-third psalm.

"Your father is a jerk! He wouldn't let me die," Joanne screamed. I looked at my father and saw him. Maybe for the first time. "Do unto others as you would . . ."

Taking Joanne's good hand in mine, I looked full into her face for a moment, then bent down and kissed her on the cheek that could still feel. Her body relaxed. A single tear slid down her face, and I felt her squeeze my hand slightly. I looked at my dad. I was my father's daughter after all.

◆ ◆ ◆

# Sis

## *Barbara R. Murrin*

I WAS the new music teacher in the community school. And when I first met them, he was in eighth grade and she in grade five.

It didn't take the common last name to tell me they were brother and sister. I could tell by that love-hate relationship so peculiar to siblings.

As the school year progressed I watched them. I saw the way she'd hang around him, trying to get his attention, while it was clear he'd just as soon she got lost and stayed that way. At times her need for attention turned her into a real pest, and he'd react by yelling at her. Sometimes she'd pretend it didn't matter; other times I knew she thought she hated him.

Grade eight isn't exactly prime time for boys physically, but she didn't know that. He was her idol: mature, sure of himself, popular.

She, on the other hand, was a somewhat awkward collection of too-big feet, teeth that would need braces, and a body that hadn't hit puberty. The face that promised to be striking in a few years still had the undeveloped curves of a child, and her experiments with her hair were less than successful. All in all, I could see that being his sister wasn't easy for her.

Halfway through the school year I announced that I was starting a beginner band. She was one of the first to sign up. To my surprise, she didn't choose flute or clarinet, as did most of the girls. She didn't even choose trumpet, the instrument her brother played. She chose French horn.

Her father told me he thought it would be a good idea for her to play an instrument different from what anyone else played. That way, he said, she would be more likely to be included in elite groups. Still, I wondered whether the need to be accepted as important in her own right wasn't the reason behind her decision. Her brother was already first chair trumpet, so how could she compete with that?

She was determined to learn her instrument, though she didn't always see the connection between learning and practicing. Sometimes she looked almost hostile as she took her place in the group of beginners and opened her music.

As the weeks passed, an interesting phenomenon developed. The more proficient she became on her instrument, the more her brother mentioned her to me. "Man, I don't know how my sister can play the French horn," he told me one day with a shake of his head. "The notes are so close together, you can almost play a whole scale with one finger." It was the first time I'd heard him express admiration for his sister.

It was obvious he hadn't told her, though, for she was still trying to earn his approval. The only difference was that now she was channeling her energy into learning an instrument rather than bugging him while he was trying to impress the girls.

Then came the big day the band students had been looking forward to. Spring concert. It was only three and a half months since the beginner band had started, but they were scheduled to make their first public appearance that night. They were terrified.

My heart went out to those beginners as I watched them polish their instruments, check their music, and readjust their reeds countless times. They came back again and again to check their tuning. They tried to joke with each other, only their stories weren't funny, and their laughter was brittle. Not even the good-natured insults could hide the trembling hands and legs.

Suddenly this sister came rushing up to me, a piece of creased paper in her hand. Her dark eyes were shining with tears, her face glowing as though she'd seen a vision. She shoved the paper into my hand and said, "Read this."

"You're probably scared to death tonight," the note said. "I remember what it was like the first time I played in public. I was scared too. Just remember, the worst thing that can happen is that you'll blow it. So take a walk and remember to breathe deep when you get up there. You'll do good." The bottom line of the scrawling was her brother's name.

"I can't believe it," she said in an awed voice. Her arms were clamped on her waist, and a tear escaped down one cheek. "It's from my brother!"

My throat tightened at the caring that had prompted him to do this for his sister. I handed the note back to her. "He's very proud of you," I said, feeling my own tears.

She smoothed the note reverently before folding it again. "Yes," she said. "I never knew that before."

I put my arm around her shoulders and began to guide her back to the other students. It was almost time for the beginners to make their debut. "You play your heart out for him tonight, understand?"

She nodded eagerly. "Oh yes!" she said. "We'll do good, won't we?"

"Of course you will," I said. And they did.

It was only one night in their lives, but it had a lasting effect on that brother and sister. Maybe they don't remember all the details, but the thoughtfulness of the older brother helped cement their relationship.

Sure, there's still competitiveness and bickering between them. But there's also a sensitivity that wasn't there before. Better still, there's a new confidence in each other. She seems more sure of herself. Part of it comes from increased maturity; part of it from knowing that, to her brother, she's a worthwhile individual.

I still watch them. I can't seem to help it. Someday he'll need her support as much as she needed his that marvelous night. And I hope she'll have the sensitivity to know when that time comes, and the caring to match his.

♦ ♦ ♦

# Love Light

## *Eleanor Friesen*

SOME kids have difficulty combining the concepts of father and love. Especially if the kids are teenagers, as my sister and I were. Especially if the father is very strict, which ours was. We thought he was just about the strictest father in the entire universe.

Not only did we have to be home by 10:30 on Saturday nights, but we usually didn't get to go anywhere in the first place.

Church socials and programs were grudgingly allowed; most home parties were definitely out; hanging around with friends after dark and board games with dice were invented by the devil and definitely not to be tolerated. In fact, according to Dad, most of our friends fell in the latter category. Since these friends' fathers never put the same restrictions on their kids, I began to suspect that our father didn't love us very much, and deep inside my heart a spot as cold as our Canadian winters began to freeze and spread.

So it came as a pleasant surprise that when a lady in our church organized a youth choir with practice on Friday nights, we were encouraged to go. Dad did like music. Since we had no car, this meant a round-trip walk of five miles. We walked it gladly, savoring the freedom of being away from home. Of course, when winter weather came and a couple of good-looking young men from the choir restricted that freedom by suggesting that we ride with them in their half-ton truck, we made no objection. Neither did Dad, except for some prolonged mumbling to no one in particular.

One star-studded evening in early spring when choir practice was over, my sister and I allowed these young men to persuade us that there was a new logging road up the mountain that would take us to our home down in the valley. We obligingly ignored the fact that in early spring logging roads become notorious for their mudholes, and it was not long before we were in one, but good.

As we stood by the side of the muddy truck watching the boys' cheerful efforts to get unstuck, I envied their lack of concern over the lateness of the hour, and began to worry about what was going to happen to us if we ever got home. Since my sister wouldn't look at me, I knew that she was worried too. There could be a lot of yelling for starters, and anything could happen after that. Like maybe choir practice becoming off-limits to us. The anger inside me froze a few more vital organs.

It took many armloads of tree branches in the mud under the back wheels before the truck finally lurched out of the muck. Somehow we got turned around and started back toward home.

As we topped the last rise one-half mile from our house, we saw a little light bobbing toward us through the darkness. I looked at my sister; she looked at me. We knew instantly what the light was. After a hard week's work and already walking six miles to get home that evening, Dad was coming on foot with the barn lantern to find us. Kerosene barn lanterns do not have very bright lights, but the beams from that one cut like a laser straight to the frozen barrens in the bottom of my soul.

Surprisingly, when we pulled up beside him, Dad calmly lifted his light so that he could see us inside, then climbed into the back of the truck for the short ride home. He quietly accepted our lame excuses about the logging road, blew out the light in the lantern, and went to bed.

He probably slept well, knowing that his children were safe at home. My sister lay very quietly in the bed beside me. I spent several wakeful hours, thinking about mudholes, and fathers, and lights bobbing in the darkness.

◆ ◆ ◆

# Secret Likeness

*Andy Demsky*

THE rain had come as predicted. Will stuffed his laundry bag with old 501s and watched the rain fill the air like smoke. The dean's stupid black terrier bounced across the wet grounds, sniffing at an occasional tree. Then it stopped abruptly and pivoted its face each way, dingbat fascination covering its hairy, toilet roll head. It sat and stared at something in the grass. Through the film of moisture on the window, Will could see the sidewalks had grown grayer in the rain and the tree trunks had all turned black.

*Will Church*

Taking hold of the white canvas bag, he shook it violently, hoping the clothes would settle to the bottom. The jeans were heavy and took up a lot of room.

Opening the bag again, he could see there wasn't much space for the dress shirts heaped at his feet. If he didn't take the shirts with him, he'd have to wash them himself when he got back. This he didn't wish for, because the laundry room in the dorm filled his nose and eyes with floating cotton dust and smelled of rancid tube socks. The cold cement floor sloped to an iron drain grown furry with rust, and the washing machines clattered like pie pans in the wind.

No . . . the dress shirts *would* fit. He pressed them into a solid wad under his muscled arm and pulled the draw string on the bag, sealing in the stale odor. His mother, a pale, sparrow-like woman, would tenaciously wash everything when he got home. His clothes would be clean, pressed, and folded when he returned to the school.

*Will Church is subject to two weeks'*

"Will!"

He dropped the taut bag and walked to the window.

"Hey!" the voice called again.

It was Speckerman and Davis. Will nodded to the two standing a story below him in the rain that plinked like nickels on his window sill.

"Hey boozer, when you takin' off?" Davis called.

Will shrugged.

"Your dad coming?"

He nodded again and wiped a hand through his hair. The two on the ground conferred with each other for a moment and then looked up, blinking in the rain.

Speckerman asked in his mild voice, "Mind if I take Jill out while you're gone?" His smile became large and open, looking more like a yawn.

Will tugged angrily at the window.

"What're you saying?" Davis asked, water dripping off the wet, gangling sleeves of his sweatshirt.

The window suddenly broke loose and came up.

"Touch her and you're dead, Speckerman!" Will said, smirking and annoyed.

The two muttered something and laughed. As they walked off Davis said, "While the cat's away . . ." He shrugged and concluded, "It's the law of the jungle."

Speckerman and Davis disappeared like two ducks into the tumbling sheets of rain. Will closed his window again and wrote *Jerks* with his finger in the moisture.

*Will Church is subject to two weeks' suspension on suspicion*

The red numerals on his alarm clock read 11:38. Will walked to the closet and looked around to be sure nothing would be left behind. Something always got left behind.

He turned and looked about the room. His old Nikes he could leave. He was wearing his Reeboks, so footwear was covered. The other essentials: blow dryer, deodorant, *Car and Driver,* Jill's 8 x 10. All had been stowed for the journey home.

Now the wait. Now the wondering. His mind wandered to the phone call home. It had been a delicate one.

"Two weeks?" his father had asked after the circumstances had been explained.

"Two big weeks," Will had said.

The expected fury had not come. The phone had been quiet for a moment.

"If you want, you can go with me on my Portland trip. I'll be there four days. Gonna build another church up in that area. I could get you on the flight if you want to go. 'Course, I'd need to know right away."

"Yeah," Will had responded.

But time alone together is what Will did not want. Three years at the boarding school, and his father was a stranger. Will couldn't weather the emotional melodrama of father-repairs-defective-son. He didn't want the ordeal of his father's diversionary Aggie jokes and his abrupt seizures of anger.

Will expected his father's usual vacillation—beginning as an anxious friend and transforming into an outraged authority. There was a line between friendly persuasion and reckless supremacy that his father crossed with bizarre agility. It defied defense and left little room for escape.

So Will sat on the corner of his bunk bed, leaning against the post dreading and dreading and dreading.

"Will!" a tin voice called from the wall speaker.

"Yeah."

"Your dad is waiting in the lobby."

"All right."

Will stood and kicked at the freestanding laundry bag.

*Will Church is subject to two weeks' suspension on suspicion of drinking alcohol.*

On occasions of this sort, there is much made about the

prudent arrangement of luggage. Even though the rain continued its steady earthward course, father and son spent a great deal of thoughtful time placing and replacing Will's three bags. Each doing his best not to insult the intelligence of the other by overzealously suggesting alternate placements of the luggage. Finally, the careful negotiations were complete. The trunk slapped wet to its locked position and sprayed the pants of father and son.

The drive began with wise observations about the weather: how it had changed over the past 20 years. It rains more now than it used to. The summers are hotter, humidity is way up, the crickets are louder, nights are colder, crops die more easily, and it's all due to the ominous movement of the jet stream, which Will pictured as a long white, narrow cloud that jets attached themselves to while ripping through the atmosphere.

The old Mr. Church went on in his angst over the gradual deterioration of the earth's ecosystem, while Will drifted off into dreams of doing loopty loops around the jet stream, cranking it up to about Mach 10, scaring the living Geritol out of his father in the copilot seat.

"Hey, I got one for you," his father said loudly, with a smile that hovered just above anguish. "How many Aggies does it take to eat an armadillo?"

"I don't know," Will said.

"Two." Laugh, laugh. "One to eat and one to direct traffic." Laugh, laugh. Then came the slippery change. The father's old face grew still. "Will, I've been thinking a lot about what happened."

"Uh-huh."

There followed a long, cumbersome silence. Will imagined his father fishing for the key, listening to the tumblers, trying to unlock Solomon's hidden solution to this one—torn between a resigned that's-my-boy slap on the behind or fire from the holy mountain.

Will imagined the aging man at home the night before thumbing through *Cruden's Concordance* muttering, "P, p, p,—ah, here it is, punishment." He could picture the spotted hands wrapping together, pressing tightly, hoping to wring out a drop of wisdom—an iota of insight.

His father, with grave drama, searched for studied answers to the thorny situation of life. For Will's edification he would put on a great moral show—Theater of the Damned—searching and agonizing over the right fatherly path to follow. But when push came to shove, after the thoughtfulness, after the Aggie jokes, came a fireworks of threats and ultimatums.

Will waited through the silence, making preparation for the fiery furnace. More than a mile went by. Will glanced at his father's salt-and-pepper gray hair from the corner of his eye. His father was ashen and motionless.

Finally Will spoke. "What is it, Dad?"

There came a gasp from the old man. His large, ancient shoulders shook, and his face grew red as a sunset. Will's insides went sick and sour.

"Are you all right?"

The old man nodded his head, and he placed his big spotted hand on Will's hand. "Maybe I haven't been fair," he whispered.

Will's father took a deep breath and kept his eyes fixed on the road. "You're like me, Will. I've hidden that from you because I had hoped to make you better than myself. But you're just like me."

Will didn't respond for a moment, collecting his thoughts. An aching, knotted lump had come to his throat at the sight of his proud father weeping openly.

"What do you mean?" Will asked.

"It's been my secret." He wiped his eyes. "I've never told you this. Your mother doesn't even know, so let's keep this between us."

"All right, Dad."

"When your father was in college, he got kicked out for drinking. He used to go into town and sneak back drunk as a monkey. In those days you were just plain kicked out." His eyes shone like glass. "I think it broke your grandpa's heart. And he punished me. It's one of the reasons I didn't finish college."

He looked at Will through bloated eyes. "I can't punish you, Will. I can't make you better than me. It's like the blind leading the blind. Please go to God. He hasn't got a temper. He's not gonna make you feel small."

Will asked, "You're not angry?"

"I can't be angry, Will. It'd be a farce. I'm just like you."

The car crested a long hill. Before them lay a wide, endless green valley, and before and above them the sky was vast and blue where the rain clouds had broken up. Far past the blue lay the great cold universe, with the galaxies and quasars and gas-lit nebulae that had rolled off the fingertips of God. They faced this, father and son, together as equals on a world in decline.

And the young Church looked into the eyes of the old Church and knew they could be friends because they were both frail and in need of something great that lay beyond the blue skies of this world.

The old Church looked into the eyes of the young Church and saw a vitality and an honest searching for things that he had long ago laid aside. And the old Church knew the young Church would grow old in grace and prosperity with the help of Someone more powerful than he. For it takes a power that creates worlds to shape the human heart.

And the two Churches traveled together that day, without suspicion or conceit, as two can, and reached their home that evening sorry they hadn't worked through the secret a long time before.

♦ ♦ ♦

# PARABLES

"*And he taught them many things by parables . . .*"
(Mark 4:2, NIV).

Why is the Bible like aerodynamic theory? How could
a professional wrestling match possibly teach a spiritual
lesson? Who has (or has not) slipped into a mucky
swamp?

From the gripping opening of "The Climber" to the
jarring conclusion of "My Song," these parables act as
light shafts in a darkened room. Our world is focused and
stretched, and a fresh vision emerges.

He who has eyes, let him see.

◆ ◆ ◆

# The Climber

## *Maylan Schurch*

ONE step and my left foot was on the solid ledge;
another, and the ledge turned rotten. My weight
had swung too far out, and there sprang into my
chest the great panic of the climber who knows
that he is about to fall, and that no matter how
much he scrambles and screams and prays he will continue to fall,
tumbling and bumping and bouncing down the mountainside to
smash to death in some dark crevasse below.

The ledge broke, and my foot kicked savagely down. I tipped,
and the sun and the sky and the mountain wheeled twice around
me. I made no sound, because I thought I was dead.

But then my chest was caught and squeezed by a rough fork
of branches, leaves slapped my face, and after a great shuddering
had stopped I saw that I was caught in a gnarled bush growing
from the cliff below the ledge.

I twisted my head and looked downward, and far below I saw

misty-green meadows and a silver river. Around and above me was the blue afternoon sky.

I called and called, and each time I released my breath I felt like I was slipping and each time I gulped in more air my chest pained. I called until my voice was raw, and still I rattled the breath in my throat in case someone should hear.

But the rest were far from me. In early afternoon I had dawdled behind them and then slipped away along an ascending path, delighting in the sunshine, trailing a nimble goat for a while, scarcely looking down, always climbing. And then I had reached that narrow ledge, and taken one false step.

And now, since there was nothing to do but see the meadow darken and the sun depart, I watched them to take my mind off the pain in my chest and the numbness in my lower body. Once I tried to move to get more comfortable, but a heart-stopping *crack* among the branches warned me not to move again.

I looked down again. A shadow covered the meadow below. I fancied I saw something moving by the river. Were the others there already? I called out to them, gathering the shreds of my voice and sending scream after painful scream down into the valley. But how could anyone hear?

*"Don't move,"* said a familiar quiet voice above me.

Great spurts of blood flooded into the veins of my ears. My heart leaped to the voice, and I twisted among the branches.

"Don't move," said the voice again. There was a scraping above me, and I felt cool gravel and a few sharp stones strike my head.

"Don't struggle." The voice was very close now. "I'm almost there. I'm going to lift you up. Do not struggle. Do you understand?"

And I felt His hand clutch my fleece. I was lifted, and my hooves crushed against His chest as He embraced me, and together we sobbed in the night.

◆ ◆ ◆

# Catching the Flight
## *Bob Prouty*

HELLO. Is this the travel agency?"

"Yes, it certainly is. How may we help you?"

"Well, I'm not sure, but I've been planning to leave on a major trip and I thought maybe you could give me some information."

"All right. Where are you hoping to go?"

"Heaven."

"Heaven, eh? Well, that's not a very common destination these days."

"Yeah, I know, but I've been booked on a special charter."

"Just a minute. Let me check . . . No, I'm sorry, sir. According to our information, that isn't possible. There are no private charters to that destination. The only way you can get there is to travel United."

"United! You're kidding! I thought this was some kind of private deal. You know, where you join up six months ahead of time and get special privileges."

"That's not what our files say, sir. No, it's very clear. This flight is open."

"You mean I might be sitting beside someone I don't know?"

"That is correct, sir."

"Don't you have any special sections?"

"I'm afraid not, sir."

"Well, what about baggage? I hear you can't take it with you."

"I don't believe I can confirm that, sir. In fact, our files indicate that you have no choice but to take it with you, at least for certain types of baggage—hopes, loves, character—that sort of thing."

"What about pet theories and sacred cows? I'd sure hate to leave those behind."

"Our information is that they would put you over the weight limit, sir."

"Well, what can you tell me about departure time?"

"Just a minute. I'll check . . . H'mmm. It seems that the flight was scheduled for departure some time ago, but there has been a delay."

"I *know* there's been a delay! That's why I'm calling. What I want to know is why the flight is being delayed."

"They're waiting for another passenger."

"For another passenger! Listen, I'm a busy man. Now, just because somebody's fouling things up, I can't—"

"Sir—"

"And let me tell you something else. This whole package isn't what I was expecting. I don't know if—"

"Excuse me, sir . . ."

"What? What?"

"Would your name be de Seah by any chance?"

"Yeah, sure, de Seah. That's me. Leo de Seah."

"I thought so. About the flight, sir . . ."

"Yes?"

"They're waiting for *you*."

◆ ◆ ◆

# The Peasant and the Industrialist

## G. W. Target

ONCE upon a time, not more than a month ago, there was a very poor peasant living in an underdeveloped country a few thousand miles from here. The sun was hot; he had worked hard in the field all morning, and his dinner of bread and cheese and goat's milk made him feel as sleepy as it always did. And so he took a little nap in the shade of the old tree under which his father used to take his naps when he was a young man.

To this underdeveloped country came a very rich industrialist from a technologically advanced nation just a few blocks from here. He was on an important fact-finding mission to establish the possibility of injecting a massive sum of investment capital into the economy, or building a giant hydroelectric power system, or the latest type nuclear generator, or a chemical plant, or an oil refinery, or something.

The sun was hot; he had just been driven 137 miles in exactly one hour and 58 minutes to find a few more facts or whatever. His expense-account luncheon at the only five-star hotel this side of the mountains had been atrocious (the soup too salty, the fish not salty enough, the steak fatty, the vegetables frozen and not fresh, the peaches and cream unfit for pigs, the coffee undrinkable, and the wine not chilled to the correct temperature for that particular vintage), and when he saw that poor peasant sleeping under the shade of that old tree it all got too much to bear.

"Stop the car!" he shouted to the driver.

He got out, stormed across the road as fast as his heart condition would allow, and woke the very poor peasant up by shouting: "What the blazes do you think you're doing!"

The very poor peasant was naturally extremely confused at being awakened like that, especially as he had been dreaming of his sweetheart and their wedding, which was to take place at the end of the harvest. But he was as polite as anybody could be under the circumstances.

"I beg your pardon, sir?"

"What the blazes do you think you're doing?" shouted the very rich industrialist.

"I was taking a little nap in the shade of the old tree under which my father, God rest him, used to take his naps when he was a young man," said the very poor peasant, thinking it ought to have been obvious what he was doing there.

"Asleep?" shouted the very rich industrialist. "Don't you know there's work to be done?"

"Work?" said the very poor peasant. "Have I not worked all—"

"You don't know the meaning of the word!" shouted the very rich industrialist—who, as you will have noticed, was a man much given to shouting, even though it made him quite short of breath. "If you people were to get hold of yourselves, change your ways, work harder and longer, you might be able to save money, invest it in some profitable little business, branch out into new lines, take on a few hands, install plant, machinery, automation, get capital in back of you, build up your interests, buy out your competitors, corner the market, climb to the top of the heap, get up and go, make your mark in the world, really *be* somebody!"

"Is it permitted to ask what I would do then, sir?" said the very poor peasant—who, though still polite, had hardly understood much of this.

"Do?" shouted the very rich industrialist, unable to believe his ears. "Do? Why, you could delegate responsibility to subordinates! Relax! Take it easy for a change! Live on the income! House in the country. Long vacations! Enjoy the fruits of your labors! Good food! Pretty girls! Soak up a little sunshine!"

"Sir," said the poor peasant. "My house is already in the country, the bread baked by my mother is the envy of every woman in the district, our cheese is the best cheese of any place in the wide world, my sweetheart is prettier than any girl I have ever seen . . . and was I not asleep in the sunshine when you woke me?"

◆ ◆ ◆

# Thornflower

## *Skip Johnson*

ONCE a tree stood beside a road. Every day men and women, boys and girls, and animals passed by.

The tree said, "They will break my branches! They will climb my boughs! They will pluck my leaves! What shall I do to protect myself?" And the tree grew long sharp thorns that would wound the hand of any who dared to touch. Then the tree felt safe, for no one came near.

But one day a man came from the city and stopped at the tree. He looked and laughed when he saw the thorns. And he drew a sword and slashed a bough and took away the long shoots, all barbed and cruel. And the tree bled and cried and cursed the man who had wounded its side and stolen its shoots.

Later when the sun was high, a crowd came from the city. A man moved in the midst of it. The tree forgot his own wounds in pity for the man. He was wounded too, and bleeding. And suddenly the tree trembled in shame, for on the man's brow were pressed down the tree's own thorns—the thorns it had grown to wound and pierce the passerby.

Then the man was gone.

The tree thought and thought from spring until fall. And when autumn came and it dropped its leaves on the ground for winter, it dropped its thorns as well, one by one.

And in the springtime in place of thorns bloomed beautiful crimson blossoms.

◆ ◆ ◆

# The Mortal, the Swamp, and the Christians

## *Jim Ayars*

THE nasty old swamp was a pretty good swamp, as swamps go. He had everything a swamp could ask for—lots of muck, quicksand in all the strategic places, slippery paths lined with dead trees and, of course, stagnant water. And how he stank!

One day the swamp was just sitting there bubbling methane when a mortal went by. *H'mmm*, thought the swamp. But that's all he thought. Mortals were always going by. So the swamp settled down and bubbled some more. He hadn't bubbled long, however, when the mortal passed by again, and again, and still again.

*This is getting monotonous*, thought the swamp. Obviously the poor mortal was lost and going in circles. Noticing that his marsh gas supply was running low, and having built up quite a taste for delicate, sweet mortals, the swamp decided it was a good time to replenish his supply.

So the swamp set about the delicious task of swallowing a mortal. He had done it dozens of times. He'd just tip one of the paths slightly and let the mortal slip into the muck. Then he'd settle back and let the mortal turn into swamp gas. It was as easy as that.

The next time the mortal passed, the swamp followed the plan. *Schloop!* Into the muck slipped the mortal. This mortal wasn't willing to die without a fight, though. He began screaming and grabbing for branches and logs. But the swamp was an old hand at swallowing mortals. He had picked a place of no escape.

Meanwhile, at the edge of the swamp on a sunny knoll a small group of Christians busily fanned a little campfire under a big pot of theology. They'd been trying all day to come up with some new recipes. Tired of the old staples, they wanted some exciting new dishes.

Lazily leaning against a maple while reading his recipe book, one Christian thought he heard a *schloop* and then a scream for help.

"H'mmm," he mumbled to himself. "Sounds like someone has fallen into the swamp." He walked over and looked into the swamp. Spying the struggling mortal, he ran back to the group shouting, "Someone has fallen into the swamp!"

All the Christians ran to see.

"Yup! Sure looks like someone has fallen into the swamp!" they exclaimed.

Then they gathered into a circle and began a heated discussion. Some said one thing. Others said another. Pretty soon they voted, and the leader solemnly rose and said, "We have agreed that someone has fallen into the swamp."

Everyone cheered. That was their first agreement of the day. How exciting! They all settled down to search their recipe books to see whether there was any reference to mortals falling into swamps.

After a few minutes one Christian shouted, "I've found it! Hohodone 5:12 says, 'Three years after the opening of the fifteenth ivy leaf a mortal shall fall into the swamp.'"

All the Christians checked their history books and hourglasses. Sure enough, it was the third year after the opening of the fifteenth ivy leaf. They shouted for joy and settled back to discuss the implications of this amazing prophecy.

After a few minutes someone suggested, "Why don't we help the poor mortal?"

So once again all the Christians huddled to discuss the new idea. After they voted, the leader stood and announced, "We have voted and decided that we should study our recipe books and discover whether helping mortals is a part of our creed."

So they settled down again, and after several minutes of monotonous mumbling punctuated by furiously flipping pages, another Christian cried, "Here it is. Evangelion 3:11 says, 'All Christians must help other mortals who fall into swamps.'"

Everyone voted excitedly, and then the leader declared, "In the light of the evidence, we must strive to help this poor mortal who is sinking in the swamp."

At that everyone ran to the edge of the swamp and began thinking of ways to help the sinking mortal. After reading quickly through a chapter in his recipe book, one Christian began chanting his favorite getting-mortals-out-of-the-swamp slogan: "When your feet are sinking low, and you would to dry land go, Jesus saves."

But the poor mortal had muck in his ears and thought that the Christian had shouted something about "don't make waves." He sank a little deeper.

Another Christian stood tall, and flailing a pharisaic finger, declared in stentorian tones, "You dumb mortal! You turned left instead of right at the fourth swamp. You knew, but you wanted your own way. Now you're suffering the consequences."

The sinking mortal, of course, was very glad to know that. But he sank a little deeper.

Another Christian knelt and prayed to the Great Spirit: "O, Great Spirit, make a tree fall 12 inches to the left of the poor mortal sinking in the swamp, that he might pull himself to safety and repent of his evil ways."

No tree fell.

Another Christian strode to the edge and with an ivory smile said, "If you ever have any trouble getting out of the swamp, come up to my office. I'll be glad to talk it over with you."

But the mortal was under a tight schedule at the moment and his work was sucking him under. He only sank a little deeper.

Another Christian hurriedly collected little branches and a log or two and began tossing them toward the poor mortal. Some went too far, others not far enough. Some sank, while others caught in overhanging tree branches. Finally he found a hollow log and filled it with proof texts, tracts, and a few whatnots. With a mighty heave the Christian tossed the missile, which hit the sinking mortal on the head. And he sank deeper still.

Another Christian came to the theology feeds—usually late. Considered strange by the rest, his main excuses for his seeming disinterest in the vital theological issues percolating in the theology pot were that he was either talking with a sinner or drawing a swamp map. He was late again this time. But as soon as he learned the trouble, he ripped off his shirt and tossed aside his polished shoes. Grabbing a nearby rope, he tied one end around a tree and the other around himself. To the slack-jawed horror of the rest, he strode manfully into the muck. With difficulty he finally reached the sinking mortal.

Grasping the mortal's upstretched hands, he pulled with all his strength, and managed to drag him to a nearby log. Clearing the mud from the wretch's eyes, he smiled and said, "I've found the Way. Come along with me."

◆ ◆ ◆

# Lukas and Mike and Me

*Maylan Schurch*

HOW come you know so much about him?" I ask Mike, my manager. He is crouching behind me, knuckling the kinks out of my shoulders.

"I know him from way back," Mike says over the crowd noise. "Back when pro wrestling was just getting started."

"He doesn't look so tough."

"Don't let his baby face and golden locks fool you." Mike fingers my ribs like he is playing a Steinway. "He's tougher than you are. You're dead if you don't pull that move I showed you."

"Right." I look across the ring at Lukas the Lion. Just like the beast he took his name from, his hair and beard are dark gold, and he wears a maroon cape with spangles. But his blue eyes look so sweet and innocent.

*"Ladies and gentlemen, in this corner . . ."*

I do three or four squat-thrusts as the announcer goes through his routine. Then *clang* goes the bell, and Mike holds me by the throat for a final instant. "Remember my move," he says into my ear. And then I shake him off, and suddenly I'm out there on the canvas facing the blond giant.

*What is wrong with this Lukas?* I ask myself as we circle each other. There's something funny about how he moves.

Then I figure it out. His legs seem stiffer than normal. He sways as he walks, stumping back and forth in front of me.

"Oh, great," I say to myself, "I've got to wrestle with a cripple."

And while I'm pitying him, and pitying Mike for being such a fool, and pitying myself for having to decide whether to stomp on this cherub-faced cripple or get out of the ring as gracefully as I can, Lukas the Lion seizes me by the hair and slams me, facedown, onto the canvas.

I leap hotly to my feet. Pity leaves me, and along with it Mike's number one rule: *Don't get mad.* I tackle Lukas and clamp his shockingly hard abdomen in my notorious "suffo-hug."

But instead of quietly going to sleep, as wrestlers usually do when I give them the "suffo-hug," Lukas inhales sharply, and I lose my grip. Then he seizes me by my trunks, spins me like a top, and again smashes me facedown onto the canvas.

*Clang!* Back in the corner Mike squirts water over my bloody chin. "You got mad," he says, "and you forgot my move." He pries open my eyelids and looks into my soul. "Do you still remember how it goes?"

I nod groggily. "But who *is* that cripple, anyway?"

"He and I go way back," says Mike. "He's strong—he's the best fighter on the planet—but he hurt himself a long time ago, and now he can't bend his knees at all."

"But he can sure body-slam."

"Yeah." Mike is watching Lukas's corner. "Don't let him set you up for a body-slam."

"Now you tell me."

"I told you before," Mike says patiently. "Trust me; remember my move, and you've got him."

*Clang.* Out on the canvas the world's still a bit flickery, Lukas hard to focus on. In he comes, and again and again I dance back. In he comes again. Apparently Angel Face wants a quick kill, and as I dodge away I feel his horrible grip for an instant on my trunks.

Come on, bell.

In he comes, knocks my arms away like women's arms, goes for a front choke, and gets it. An orchestra begins to play between my ears.

*Remember Michael's move.*

Never has the move seemed sillier. In seconds I'll be out, downed in two rounds. The move seems so self-defeating.

But Lukas's angelic face is turning a splotchy fireworks-maroon before my bulging eyes, and I have to do something.

So I do Mike's move. A quick drop to my knees, crouching low, relaxing. And then I feel the iron hand miraculously release, hear a howl above me, and as the blood thunders back into my neck and head and ears, Lukas the roaring Lion slams to the canvas by my side.

♦ ♦ ♦

# Gooley Flies Again

*Joseph Bayly*

MY roommate is a guy named Gooley. Herb Gooley. He transferred to this crummy little school in the boondocks about six months ago. When he first arrived, we all were asking why he came here from that other college at the beginning of his senior year. Everybody's heard of it; nobody's heard of us.

Only thing we have that they don't have is—this is a flight school. A crummy flight school. What they have and we don't have would fill a book.

One night I ask Herb straight out, "Why did you come here?"

"One reason," he says. "Last Christmas vacation I learned to fly. When I returned to campus, I was a freak—an honest-to-goodness freak. Nobody but me knew how to fly. So I decided to switch to flight school, a place where everyone could fly. That's why I'm here."

I should explain that I don't mean flying planes, or gliders, or balloons, or flying anything. I mean we can fly, period.

We can step out of a window, and we're airborne. I remember my first flight—it was while I was still in high school—off a barn in the Blue Ridge Mountains. Some of the guys and girls here have been flying ever since they were little kids.

So the reason Herb Gooley gave for coming here made sense. (Except for one thing, which he couldn't have known before he came, the sort of thing you don't learn from reading a school catalog.)

Gooley is a sensitive guy, withdrawn, doesn't talk to many people. But there's a reason for how he is: For one thing, he got off to a bad start. I've never seen a happier freshman than Gooley was when he first showed up. I don't mean that he was actually a freshman—like I said, he was a transfer senior. But he had that same stupid innocence.

It was one of those hot afternoons in September, like so many days when school just begins. I was stripped to the waist, arranging my new clothes on hangers, when this new student comes through the window. He flew in—our room is on the third floor of Flescher Hall.

"I'm Herb Gooley," he says. "Boy, have I ever been looking forward to coming here."

"To this crummy school? Why?"

He looks sort of surprised. "Why? Because it's a flight school. You can fly, can't you? The other guys in this dorm can fly, can't they? And the girls—just think of having a flying date. Wow!"

He dumps his bags on the floor and pumps my hand.

I wonder, should I tell him straight off, or should I let him find out for himself? I guess I'm sort of chicken, because I decide not to say anything. Let someone else tell him.

"Yeah, this is a flight school, all right. We can all fly, including the profs and the administration; the public relations department too. So you can have that bed over there by the door, Gooley, and that dresser, and either closet—except that I've got my things in this one."

He doesn't say anything, but begins to unpack. First thing out of his suitcase is a copy of *Aerodynamic Theory*. It goes on his desk.

Around 5:30 I head for the dining hall. "Coming along?" I ask.

"Not yet," Gooley says. "Don't wait for me. I want to finish here first. I'll be along before it closes."

So I walk on over and go through the cafeteria line. I find my crowd and sit down to eat with them.

We're on dessert when there's a little stir over by the door.

"What do we have here?" someone says.

"An exhibitionist."

"A new student, you can tell that. Nobody else would fly on campus."

Sure enough, it's Herb Gooley, my new roommate. He comes through the door and gently touches down by the stack of trays and the silver holder. He's got a smooth technique.

Everybody gets sort of quiet. I don't know about the others, but suddenly I'm thinking about some of my flights in high school days.

"You're too late," this battle-ax who runs the cafeteria says. "We close at 6:30."

The clock on the wall says 6:30. She's right, which is what she always is.

"Serves him right," a girl going back for seconds on milk says, loud enough for Herb to hear. "He's just a show-off."

Gooley looks sort of hurt, but he doesn't say anything. He just heads out the door, walking.

"He'll learn," someone at my table says. "We all learned."

And he did, during the following weeks.

First thing he found out was that here nobody flies. In spite of this being a flight school, and everyone can fly (theoretically), we're all grounded.

There's a lot of talk about flight, of course—flight courses, references to flight in a lot of other courses, a daily flight hour—but nobody flies.

Some of us came here planning to be flight instructors. I myself wanted to teach Africans how to fly, but it didn't last long.

Actually, the deadest things are the flight courses. They use *Aerodynamic Theory* as the text, but you'd never recognize it. One flight out of a hayloft has more excitement to it than a year of that course.

One night we got into a discussion on our floor of the dorm.

"Look, Gooley," one of the guys says, "tell us about the college you were in before you came here. Is it true that they have more exciting courses than we do here?"

"A lot of them, yes," Gooley says. "But they don't know anything about how to fly."

"Are the girls real partiers?"

"I guess so. But they can't fly."

The way Herb answers sort of frustrates the guys who are asking the questions, because they probably would jump at a chance to transfer to the school he came from.

"I think this flying isn't all it's cracked up to be," one of them says.

"I feel the same way," another chimes in. "And besides, it seems sort of selfish to me to fly when the rest of the world is walking."

"Not only selfish—to them you look like some kind of a nut up there above the ground. From here on, any flights I take are going to be when nobody's around to see me."

"Besides, the world needs to be taught how to walk; and pavements and roads need to be improved."

"Did any of you read John Robin's book? It's a pretty strong critique of *Aerodynamic Theory*, and he does an effective job of questioning the usual foundations of flight. The significant thing is that Robin is a flyer, not a walker."

That was the only time I ever saw Herb Gooley mad. "Ugh," he says, and dives out the window. (It was a cold night, but fortunately the window was open because the room was getting stuffy. Otherwise I think Herb would have gone right through the glass.)

He didn't return until early next morning. I heard him at the window and got up to open it. It had begun to snow, and he was covered. He looked nearly exhausted, but happier than I'd seen him since the day he first arrived.

That night marked a big change in Herb Gooley. Only, I didn't know it at the time.

He began to fly again, on campus.

Now when you're with flyers, flying isn't remarkable. Actually, it's the basic minimum, and taken for granted. What worries us is perfection, and it's sort of embarrassing, around other flyers, to try an extra little maneuver, or to stay aloft longer than usual. There can be such a letdown; and the competition is so keen. There's always someone who can fly better than you. That's one reason nobody actually flies here. At least they didn't, not until Gooley took it up again.

Like the flight prof says, "This is a school for flying, not an airport. You've come here to learn more about flying, not to fly. We want to teach you how to fly with real conviction." Then he draws diagrams on the blackboard, and walks across the campus.

Meanwhile, Herb is getting better and better. I mean his flying is improving. You can see him on a moonlit night, trying all sorts of flight gymnastics.

Moonlit nights—that brings me to another side of the change in Gooley. He began to have flying dates. Not many of the girls, except one or two, would be caught dead on a flight date, especially with Herb.

What can you talk about on a flying date? What can you do? We discuss it while Gooley's out of the dorm. He was out a lot those last months of school. Not just flying or on flight dates, but teaching a bunch of kids to fly at the community center in town and studying *Aerodynamic Theory* with a little group of students.

"Sure we can fly . . . at least as well as that guy Gooley. But after all, real life is down here on the earth. It's not as if we were birds."

"Besides, we've got to learn to relate to the walkers, and that's a lot harder to do than flying."

"I've found—I don't know about the rest of you guys—but I've found that they're not much interested in my flying ability. I mean, the walkers aren't. So it's important to show them that I can walk."

"Don't get me wrong; it's not that I'm against flying. I'm not. But you don't have to fly to be for flying."

So the year ends. We graduate.

While we're packing I ask Gooley what he plans to do next year.

"Grad school," he says, "in a walking university. You see, I was reading *Aerodynamic Theory* the other day, where it says that you can take off best against the wind."

♦ ♦ ♦

# Asking for Bread

## *Jeris E. Bragan*

ONCE there was a family who fell on hard times. They were proud and independent people, so they refused to ask anybody for help. Soon all their money was gone, and the cupboards were empty of food.

"God is our last help," the father said. "Let's pray for food." They all knelt and poured out their hearts to God.

No sooner had their prayers stopped when they heard a loud knock at the door. Everybody smiled as the father opened the door; they *knew* somebody would be there with an armload of groceries.

But nobody was there. Instead, a small box was sitting on the welcome mat. Curious, the family gathered around as the father opened the box. Their faces fell when they saw the contents: just a small rock.

"God is testing our faith," the father explained. "We'll pray again tomorrow."

They prayed more fervently the following night. Their prayers for food were punctuated by the sound of growling stomachs. Once again a loud knock greeted the end of the last prayers. The mother rushed to the door, her face covered with a tight smile. It vanished as she saw another, larger box on the mat. Inside was a slightly larger rock.

"We ask the Lord for bread and He gives us a stone," the father whispered bitterly. But he didn't give up his faith. Each night the family prayed as before, and each night the last Amen was answered by a knock on the door. The boxes kept getting larger, but the contents were always the same: a progressively heavier rock.

Finally they prayed no more. They gave up on God and waited for starvation to finish them off. Fortunately, a neighbor came by just before they perished. Ambulances hastily took each one off to the hospital, where they would be nursed back to health.

Back at the house a confused and astonished police officer wandered from room to room, looking at the yellow rocks scattered about the house. "I don't understand it," he muttered, shaking his head. "These people were starving to death while stacked all over the house was a king's ransom in pure gold!"

♦ ♦ ♦

# Four Men Who Wanted to See God

### Christopher Blake

ONCE there were four men who wanted to see God. The men lived day and night in a cold dark room surrounded by thick, towering walls. On the eastern wall, just beneath the ceiling, appeared their one source of hope.

It was a window. Each day a golden shaft of sunlight lunged through this opening and inched down the western wall. Fascinated, the men watched the light as it moved. They longed to see beyond the window to the true source of warmth; they hungered for a glimpse of the great God.

Though the opening was small—too small for a man to fit through—the four men often made heroic attempts to reach it. Each tried running and leaping against the wall, clawing desperately toward the tiny opening, but to no avail. The window was too high.

It became apparent then that the men would have to work together, so they developed a plan. Perhaps by standing one on top of another the person on top might be able to see through the window!

However, the question soon arose: Who will be the one on top? Who will be the one to see God? All realized this was the supreme desire for each man.

And so they sat, wondering.

Presently Rafael stood. "I will support you," he said, and waited for the others.

After a few moments, José slowly pushed himself up. "I will be next," he volunteered.

The remaining two sat unmoving, staring at their feet.

At last, with a sigh, Weldon rose. "I will be third," he offered.

The three men looked down at Sam. It would be Sam on top.

Now Rafael was moving toward the eastern wall. He spread

his legs, crouched, and pressed his palms against the wall. José placed one foot on Rafael and boosted himself until he stood balancing on Rafael's shoulders. Next Weldon climbed over the straining Rafael, past the struggling José until he could stand, his head just below the window.

Sam wasted no time. He scrambled over Rafael and José and, with help from Weldon, was catapulted to the opening where he thrust his head through . . . ten seconds . . . the men below trembled . . . twenty seconds . . . they puffed and groaned . . . twenty-five seconds . . . the column shook . . . twenty-eight seconds. . . .

The column collapsed. Arms and legs plummeted to a tangled heap where the men lay moaning, their eyes closed, their chests heaving. Slowly they rolled and untangled and with painful effort crawled apart to sit. From there the three men eagerly searched Sam's face, and waited for the vision.

"I saw through the window," Sam began, "and I saw many things. I saw wispy clouds laced across a bright sky. I watched speckled birds soar and wheel. There were oaks and sycamores on grassy hills and distant snow-capped mountains. I felt the wind slap and heard the rustling of leaves and I smelled salt in the air.

"I saw many things," he said again, and then he paused, gazing at the window. "But I did not see God."

The men sat huddled in silence, their heads bowed. The air was heavy. The ground seemed unusually cold and hard. Suddenly Rafael spoke.

*"I saw God."*

The others jerked and stared.

"As I shouldered the weight, the tremendous weight," Rafael continued, "as I staggered and strained under it, my muscles on fire, my eyes stinging, my mind crying out, as I carried it all for as long as I could and then longer—I saw Him."

The others sat, marveling.

*"I saw God, too."*

José's voice shattered the silence. "As I balanced between what was above and what was below, as I felt the soles pushing against my back and head, as I struggled and shifted to keep us steady, to keep us somehow pointing up—I saw Him."

The others sat, thinking.

"*I also saw God.*" It was Weldon. His eyes gleamed.

"As I approached the opening—so near—I wanted to be there myself. But it was when I stretched out my arms—so far—and lifted a friend—I saw God."

◆ ◆ ◆

# My Song
### Linda Dick

THE recital was coming.

All my friends were composing special melodies for the occasion. George was writing a solemn processional, with full, pounding chords and a solid melody line. John's new song was a love poem, flowing softly with arpeggios. Dora's dance was strong and hearty, a real foot-tapper. Susan was composing a crashing, clashing contemporary number, full of dissonance and syncopation. But I was stuck, dry of inspiration.

All semester we'd been learning chord structure and arpeggio patterns, and the art of weaving them together to make music. The Maestro had stressed, "The music you write must come from within you. Otherwise it will have no soul, and no one will want to listen to it. It will be dead tones and nothing more."

I looked into my soul and jumped back in puzzled horror. It was empty, bare. Trembling, I went to the Maestro.

"Come in, girl. Tell me what is in your heart."

I stumbled to his chair, on the verge of tears. "Maestro, there's nothing in my heart. My soul is empty."

He clicked his tongue. "Then we must fill it. Come. Look out the window at my garden. What do you see?"

The world I saw displayed an apple tree in blossom. I heard a robin's trill swelling from behind the perfumed lace of the flowers. Daffodils pushed sleepy gold heads out of rich brown beds. The soft breath of the south wind tickled the wide lawns into waves of rolling laughter. Overhead sparkled a glorious blue sky, sprinkled with powdered sugar clouds.

My empty soul was filled—with peace, with joy, with praise for the Gardener of this world. But the song sounding in my heart was far too complicated for my stiff fingers alone. I turned pleading eyes to the face of the Maestro behind me.

"Would you help me with my song?"

He took my hands in his and led me to the piano.

"Will you play a left-hand chord skeleton as I pick out the melody?" I asked, excited to start. He nodded, and we began.

My melody grew, strong and sweet. Immediately I felt more confident. I could do it. I could write my own song.

I played louder, trying to stand out more against the smooth, rhythmic background chords. But the louder I got, the more raucous and tinny my song became. My fingers began slipping, hitting false tones that clashed and rang harshly against the steady beat that the Maestro was creating.

I looked down at his strong hands on the keys and then up into his patient eyes.

"What's wrong?" I cried. "I have the melody, and you're providing my background. What's wrong?"

His answer was simple and direct. "The title."

◆ ◆ ◆

# SHARING

When Jesus said, "Freely you have received, freely give" (Matthew 10:8, NIV), what did He mean?

In "He Ain't Got No Name," learn how a banana peel can change a life. Watch a young woman live out her beliefs in "I Not Be Needing This." Listen to barriers come crashing down in a restaurant, a hospital, a crowded city bus.

These stories are for sharing.

◆ ◆ ◆

## A Feast of Doughnuts

### *Jonathan Butler*

WE wanted to do something crazy on Saturday night. We were a living room full of people tired of Scrabble and Carroms and television. About 10 of us, under 30 and over — brothers, a sister, a friend, in-laws, and parents — thought of singing Christmas carols door-to-door in June, or pasting a sign on the city water tower, or going to a restaurant to order only Alka-Seltzer.

Then we struck on *the idea*. We would infiltrate a little café in twos and threes, at odd times, until we were all seated around the counter. We would be arranged as a couple chatting, an old man sitting alone, or three friends in a row. Then our plan was to *interrelate* — to "get acquainted" as though we were total strangers getting to know one another. We would then see how the others in the place reacted.

We chose a Dunkin' Donuts café with a truck-stop atmosphere of glaring neon and bustling service and shirt-sleeved customers, without promise socially. Socially, rather antiseptic. Gradually, over 10 to 20 minutes, we arrived in three cars and filtered into the little snack shop.

We made up about a third of the clientele sitting at the horseshoe-shaped linoleum counter. We waited for our orders, talking quietly, staring at price lists or waitresses. I spoke softly to the "stranger" next to me (an in-law).

Then one of us ventured a question to the cashier. "Say, do you use *bleached* flour in these doughnuts?"

The woman looked startled by a break of the usual silence. The manager behind her flinched (we think) and came forward.

"Yes," he said warily, and offered an explanation.

Another of ours from across the counter called out, feigning confusion, "What did you say is in your doughnut? Is there something *wrong* with it?"

"No," someone else replied, "they were talking about the kind of flour in these doughnuts. You know, you can't worry too much about health these days."

The cafe was stirring, smiling, tittering with laughter. Two platinum blondes tensed up and tried to ignore the lack of sophistication.

"Of course, no food is really safe nowadays," said one of us. "Meat is diseased and vegetables are polluted."

"Come on! Things aren't that bad." The manager had relaxed with amusement.

An old woman far down the counter was heard saying, "They must be a college crowd. Do you get such a friendly bunch all the time?"

"No," said the manager, "and it beats calling the police."

Humorously, a boy suggested that we meet here again next Saturday night. We'd be the board of directors for a new health food restaurant.

"With lots of prune juice," someone said.

"And lots of restrooms," countered another.

Others were joining in. The conversation ranged from food to politics to music (there was a juke box) to how strangers never talk in strange places like a café.

We actually reflected on it then, and laughed about how this improbable conglomerate of people formed some kind of *fellowship*.

"What do you think about their building a new sports stadium?" said a young latecomer, and his father nudged him to keep quiet.

"No!" he said, "I want to know. I may never get another chance at a group like this."

Comments came from here and there, some pro and some con and some only funny. Even the reluctant blondes, whom we never prodded, finally came in, timidly and then less timidly.

We were all only too ready to listen, to laugh, to respond, as the social crescendo continued to build until no one, absolutely no one, was left out. Over Dunkin' Donuts and hot drinks we witnessed some sort of common spirit surfacing. The snack had become a feast.

In time, we began to leave as we had come in, at intervals. It would have been criminal, and perhaps sacrilegious, to reveal the "practical joke" that undergirded the evening. By this time, it was more important than a joke.

"I'm tired and I ought to go home," mused one young woman, her chin on her hands. "But I don't want to. It's too good here."

We arrived home, refilling our living room, dazed by the experience. How thin the walls that divide us from one another at ball parks and discount stores and restaurants! How paper thin.

◆ ◆ ◆

# He Ain't Got No Name
## *Tom Ashlock*

I PARKED a block away from the Greyhound bus station. I didn't see him until I opened the car door. He was sitting in the middle of his yard, staring at a spot on the pavement now blocked by my car. I realized the three-foot strip of gravel and dirt between the sidewalk and the metal front steps was his yard.

A glance at my watch showed me I had 20 minutes before the bus would be in. As I slowly squatted down I smiled and said, "Hi, Tiger, what's your name?"

He didn't smile. He didn't cry. And when his eyes met mine

they just looked but didn't say anything. *He's about 4,* I told myself.

I tried again. "Here, let's see. Shall we make a bird?" I began to arrange the gravel in front of him in an outline of a bird. He looked down for an instant, then back again. He zeroed in on my eyes. "Is your name Bobby?" I asked in a tone of voice that tried to say *"I like you."*

A girl of about 10 or 11 stepped out the open front door onto the little porch and answered, "He ain't got no name. We just keep him."

The girl and I visited for a while. Barbara was her name. As we got acquainted, she came down all but the last step. Barbara talked with her eyebrows as well as her eyes. Fifteen minutes later all I knew about the little boy was that Barbara watched him till his "gran" took him home and that "He don't say nothin' much."

When I left for the bus station Barbara waved. And "Bobby"? Well, he ain't got no name, and as I walked away his expressionless eyes left mine and again stared through my car.

Off and on for the rest of the day I could see those empty eyes and that blank face. That night in a troubled sleep I saw another child's eyes. They were dark-brown eyes set in a heart-shaped face, a face I've seen many, many times.

I had been riding on the train from Calcutta across India to the city of Bombay. The *clicketyclack, click, click* of the wheels on the rails telescoped the night into a few minutes. It was now 8:30 in the morning, and I was about to finish my breakfast with a nice large banana.

We were at a station in an unknown city. Outside were the usual sounds of hawkers selling their wares and people scurrying back and forth trying to find a place on the train. Without turning to look out the window on the side opposite the platform, I dropped my banana peeling as a kind gesture to the goats that I knew frequented the small stations in that part of India.

"Thank you, sir!" I was startled by a child's voice—clear and sweet. I looked out the window and saw that face. She was probably 9 years old, though smaller than most 6-year-olds. Her beautiful sad eyes sparkled for a fleeting moment as mine met hers. Again she said, in her language, "Thank you very much, sir"—her busy little hands brushing the cinders and dust off the banana peeling.

Suddenly the lights in her eyes went out. Terror contorted her sallow cheeks. Quickly, her hands trembling now, she began to stuff the banana peeling in her mouth. Then I saw it coming. A skeleton. No, it was a boy—maybe 12 or maybe 14—in rags, his legs and arms like broomsticks. He pounced on his victim. Slapping her to the ground, he grabbed the banana peel and with three quick bites peel, cinders, and dust were gone.

I looked toward the platform, hoping to find a banana vendor going by. No banana vendor. The train was moving now. When I looked back out the window the little girl was still sitting in the dust trying to wipe her tear-stained face with the hem of her torn rag skirt. The train turned a corner, and she was gone.

At the next station I bought two large bunches of bananas and gave them, one by one, to other hungry boys and girls.

But that face has been indelibly stamped on my mind.

It's been 31 years, and still, every once in awhile, I hear "Thank you, sir. Thank you very much, sir," and see the sparkle in those brown eyes change to terror. I have often wished that just once I would dream I'd had time to give the girl a banana. But, as always, the train rounds the corner and she's gone.

But "Bobby," I could do something for him. As I said my prayers, I promised myself I would go back down to the inner-city bus station. He would be there. Maybe "Bobby" he-ain't-got-no-name would like an ice-cream cone.

Three weeks later, a toy truck on the car seat beside me, I headed toward the bus station on 12th and New York. I slowed down in front of the row house. A for sale sign leaned against the house. The door and windows were boarded up. "Bobby" he-ain't-got-no-name was gone.

But the city is still there.

♦ ♦ ♦

# One Suffering One

## *Arthur A. Milward*

SHE didn't have red hair or freckles, but somehow she reminded me of a combination of Peppermint Patty and the little red-haired girl. She had the contrasting qualities of courage and innocent appeal.

She was about 10 or 12 years old. It was hard to be sure of her age from her appearance, as her stunted, malformed frame made her look younger than she was. But her small oval face wore an expression more appropriate to a grown woman.

Her eyes were her dominant feature. Large, dark, and luminous, fringed by long, thick lashes, they were her one beauty. She had the habit of gazing steadily for a long moment at a newcomer to the children's ward. If she liked what she saw, her face would light up and she would shuffle over and introduce herself.

She had a smile, the nurses said, that could light up a room—and could make you forget her misshapen body and painful, awkward movements.

She smiled often. I never saw her cry, although she had experienced a great deal of pain, rejection, and disappointment. Valerie, I gathered, had already shed all her tears several years and countless operations ago.

Valerie would come to the children's surgical ward for prolonged periods. Then she would disappear, only to return within a few months for further corrective surgery—surgery that could only, at best, make life manageable for her. She had MBD—multiple birth defects.

Valerie had a well-developed and slightly cynical sense of humor. When some unthinking visitor would ask what was wrong with her, she would smile sweetly and suggest that he return later when he had a day off work and time to spare. "But," she would add innocently, "if you're in a hurry, I can tell you what's right with me."

Whenever she was recovering from one of her operations, Valerie would "fall" out of her bed—which was the only way she could manage to get out of bed without help (and she scorned help). She would shuffle around the ward, helping with the care of the other children.

The small patients liked Valerie in spite of her appearance and curious method of maneuvering. She could get them to do things when the nurses failed.

Valerie stood for no nonsense. Pain was a fact of life as far as she was concerned. And she had, in her small, misshapen frame, enough courage for a wardful of children.

Valerie's parents didn't visit her every day, as many of the other children's parents did. Possibly her parents were both working or had other children to care for. They came once or twice a week, and Valerie didn't seem to care desperately whether her mother came or not. A young, fashionably dressed woman, her mother always seemed to be in a hurry. She always gave an impression of embarrassment, and she sort of disassociated herself from her daughter when other parents stopped by.

But Valerie's father was outgoing and affectionate. He would wait at the end of the ward for Valerie to shuffle across to meet him, her face lit up. He always greeted her in the same way. "Hi there, beautiful," he'd call. He made it sound as if he really meant it. And just for a moment, as the little girl reached the end of her shuffling run toward him, dropped her canes, and fell into his arms, he was right.

Then one cold and windy autumn night Billy came into the ward. Actually, it was very early in the morning, before dawn. He came up from emergency surgery, the victim of a car wreck on the M-2 expressway.

His parents were relatively unhurt, but Billy had been pinned in the wreckage for a long time. He had severe injuries to his lower legs. The doctor's prognosis was that 8-year-old Billy had taken his last steps.

Billy was sunk in deep depression. He would never walk again, let alone run, jump, play soccer, or do any of the other things that made his life worth living.

But Valerie had other ideas. After summing up the situation, she decided that the prognosis was nonsense. "The kid'll walk," she declared. She had been there. She knew.

When, fairly well along in his convalescence, Billy still refused to get out of bed, put his feet on the floor, and try to stand, Valerie took over his case. After breakfast one morning she issued her first directive. "Out of that bed, kid; it's time to get up!"

Billy tearfully protested that he couldn't walk. He demanded that she go away and leave him alone. But by sheer force of will she coaxed him out of his bed and into an upright position, then into the metal walker.

She spent exhausting hours with him every day. And at the end of the day she would crumple into an untidy heap on the floor. She would be asleep before a nurse came by to lift her onto her bed.

She put up with all kinds of abuse from her unwilling patient. Once, early on in the rehabilitation program, Billy lost his temper and stormed at her, "Valerie, why can't you leave me alone? What do you know? You're weird."

Valerie stopped dead. Her oval face went white and her chin quivered. She looked as close to tears as I ever saw her. But only for a moment. Then she stuck out her chin and fixed the boy with her eyes.

"I know it," she said. "But I can't help it—and you can! Come on." After that, things went better. Billy became more cooperative.

Some weeks later he began to share her faith that he would recover. He became enthusiastic, and the two children grew to be best friends.

Then, close to three months after he'd entered the hospital, Billy closed the curtains around his bed. He dressed himself in the new suit his excited parents had brought, packed his things into his small suitcase, and walked with his family to the parking lot in front of the hospital.

Valerie and some staff workers were there. Billy, grinning from ear to ear, turned and waved. Everyone waved back except Valerie. She couldn't. She needed both hands on her canes to support herself. Her face showed no sign of emotion, but her tiny knuckles clutching the handles of her walking canes were very white. The contrast was hard to bear. The excited, happy little boy who had learned to walk again, and the tiny, misshapen girl who would never walk properly.

Billy got into the car with his parents and young sister. And with a final wave he was gone.

Onlookers and hospital staff stood staring out into the courtyard, unwilling to move.

Valerie was the first to speak. "Well," she said, "what are we all staring at? There's work to be done. Come on, it's time to get trays round for supper."

In heaven Valerie will walk straight and tall. She will walk without tiring, and she won't fall down.

◆ ◆ ◆

# I Not Be Needing This

## *Joan-Marie Cook*

AS hard as I try, I can't remember when I first saw Annie. She was just sort of always there—a pail of sudsy water in her hands, a great, throbbing smile on her unmistakable Asian face.

Annie was more than student janitor of our college dorm; she was a kind of cleanliness campaign all by herself. The dean often said that the day Annie took over, every girl in the dorm changed. The halls, washrooms, the spacious lobby, even the basement laundry, were always gleaming. Perhaps it was some inherent respect for all lovely things that kept my friends and me from our usual careless habits. With Annie always there or sure to come soon, who could bear to drop a candy wrapper or an empty soap carton? Why, the girl would have taken it as a personal insult.

One day, sitting idly under the hair drier in the washroom, I felt a sharp sense of detachment. Here were girls I knew, busy with the endless rounds of washing, ironing, and gossiping. I could see talk moving their mouths, see the changing of their expressions, yet I could hear none of their sounds. It seemed nothing they could do would affect me, apart from them as I was. It was as if I were some strange spirit visitor.

Then, through this brief minute of fantasy, I discovered something too obvious to notice during days of reality. There was another girl in the room who, although she moved and spoke and smiled, was apart from the others. Annie, with her simple brown dress and too-big loafers, now offering sympathetic advice to a girl who had washed red pants with her undies; again, cleaning an iron for a helpless freshman.

But Annie, for all the nice things she did for people, was as much separated from them all as was I, surrounded by the screaming wind of the hair drier. And for the first time I saw her as a girl among girls, a classmate.

That night I went to visit her in her basement room. She lived alone, and her room was bare to the point of bleakness. But the thing I noticed then, and came to expect as my visits grew customary, was the huge bouquet of wild flowers that covered her desk. Annie told me that she loved going for long walks alone, and I knew she meant *long* walks, because flowers like those grew only high in the mountains surrounding the campus.

At first I was merely interested in Annie as a very unusual girl with mad tales to tell of escape from Communist forces in China. But soon I was going to her room for another reason—I liked it there. I could stretch out on her faded cloth rug and study for hours without an interruption. Annie was never bothered with visitors.

I began to notice things—the high grades she pulled in her math and science classes, her appreciation of beauty, the way she thought everything through and had reasons for each thing she did. Nothing in her life was insignificant; everything she did had meaning. There was more to Annie than the huge grin and mumbles that hid her real personality.

One evening as I lay on her rug studying, I looked up and saw Annie whispering over her book, her straight black hair pinned clumsily behind her ears. Boldness grasped me. "Let's cut your hair, Annie," I said. And to my surprise she liked the idea.

"You do it," she grinned, pulling some scissors from her desk. I was far from professional, but I gave her a simple, neat haircut and showed her how to curl her hair. The next day I was as surprised as everyone else at how pretty she looked. I was established in her eyes as something of a wonder.

I had never felt about anyone the way I felt about Annie. I wanted to make a speech in assembly; I wanted to walk up and slap people who ignored her timid attempts at friendship. I wanted to *help* her.

Because my home was in a distant state, I accepted an invitation from a girlfriend to spend spring vacation in her home. Alice's home was the most elegant I had ever stayed in.

One morning over a late, luxurious breakfast we played a "most-interesting-person" game. We each described an unusual person. I talked of Annie. Alice's teenage sister, Julie, listened carefully as I spoke. When I had finished, she left the room, although we were not through playing the game.

The next day as we were leaving for school, Alice's mother carried a huge box to the car. "Just a few things Julie doesn't need anymore," she explained. "She thought maybe Annie would like them."

I was exuberant. Back at school my roommate, Barbara, and I examined the contents of the box—sweaters, skirts, a soft blue coat, a swirling formal—every piece was exquisite. Barbara was a competent seamstress, so we decided to have Annie try on the things in our room; then in case anything needed altering, we could pin and sew there.

After supper we led Annie to our room, chattering excitedly about the surprise we had for her. Her eyes grew wider and wider with each lovely thing we took from the box. As we got out our pins and tape measure I noticed that Annie was trying to tell us something. She stood in the middle of the clothes, one frilly blouse clasped absently in her brown hand. Her manner was so awkward, so embarrassed, it seemed—and I am sure she felt this too—that we were practically strangers.

I smiled at her, and I think she realized how much I wanted to understand what she was thinking. She began shaking her head from side to side, and finally she said, "I cannot be taking these things, for I not be needing them. I have two school thing, one work thing, and one church thing."

Barbara and I laughed, relieved. "Oh, Annie, of course you don't exactly *need* them, but everyone has things she doesn't really need. It's fun to have lots of different things."

But Annie was more serious than I had ever seen her. "There be other people who not have so much as I. They should be having these. I not be needing them; I have two school thing, one work thing—"

"And one church thing, we know." Barbara was exasperated, and she couldn't hide it. "But Annie, *we* want you to have the nice things. It will make us happier."

Annie sat very still and listened thoughtfully to all our arguments. Her answer was always the same, "But I not be needing them." I knew all along it was no use. Annie liked her plain, clean dresses. They were all she needed; they were all she wanted.

Finally we persuaded her to take one brown sweater. When she left, Barbara looked at me with tears of disappointment in her eyes. "She's crazy. Everyone knows that it's materialistic to have more than you need. It's a good principle, but no one *lives* like that."

I didn't say anything. For the first time in my life my closet looked sickeningly full.

Several days passed, and then one evening I found a note under my door. The familiar scrawl said:

"I hope you not be caring, but I gave the sweater to Ressie, who works at nights at the dairy. I really not be needing it. Like I explain, I have two school thing, one work thing, and one church thing."

◆ ◆ ◆

# "Sing," She Said
## Sharon Faiola Peterson

IT wasn't all the flirting that bothered me. It was her being just a little too "cutesy"—too eager to please. You know, the kind of waitress you half expect to come out in a Shirley Temple wig and tap dance "On the Good Ship Lollipop" and right on into your heart, if it meant a bigger tip. Frankly, her neon-lit smile and dimples made me sick.

Not that I was jealous. I was used to the guys gawking and flirting. After all, an entire summer of near isolation from the opposite sex places quite a strain on eleven men. Ask any student of Freud, or student of men. For that matter, just ask any lonely pianist who plays for an all-male chorus.

No, I wasn't envious of that glazed stare in their eyes. And just because my never-had-the-guts-to-wear-before low-necklined dress went unheralded, and because Mark had just said I exuded a motherly image, those had nothing to do with it. Nothing at all.

Our waitress was flitting about from Darrell to Orvin to Tom, taking orders down like subscriptions to *Playboy*. Her little-girl voice oozed like syrup. She was so "sweet." I was just waiting for her to sit on Dennis' lap or to pinch Paul's cheek.

Laugh, laugh, laugh. Giggle, giggle, giggle. Everything she or the guys said was *so funny*. Everyone was suddenly a comedian and Denny's Restaurant the set for a situation comedy. I'd rather have been home watching *I Love Lucy* reruns, instead of in Placerville watching my men make fools of themselves.

She was partially through our orders when she noticed the team's look-alike suits.

"Oh, are you all members of a group or something?" she asked in wide-eyed wonder.

Smart. Really smart. I wondered what other brilliant deductions she'd wow us with next.

"We're all part of a Christian singing group," Keith offered. Did he have to put on such a suave voice?

"What's your name?" little Miss Denny's Darling asked.

"Well, you have to tell us yours first," Glenn piped up.

Her name could have been Siegfried for all I recall; I was deciding whether Glenn would kick me back if I laid into his shin.

"We're The Fellowship," continued Keith. "And we've been presenting musical and gymnastic programs here in Placerville for the past two weeks."

"Oh, The Fellowship! I've heard of you!" she squealed, and jumped about like an erratic cricket. "Now I recognize you," she said, pointing to Keith, who happened to be straightening his tie. "You came by the house yesterday inviting my friend and me to your meetings." Keith beamed.

"Well," she said, placing her hands on her hips, "I won't take any more orders till you sing a song for me."

The Fellowship looked at her in disbelief.

"No, I'm serious," she insisted. "Sing for your supper."

The guys looked at one another, at the crowded coffee shop,

then at Pastor Wick, who just shrugged his shoulders.

There was an awkward pause. Then they opened their mouths and began to sing.

And I closed my eyes and plotted her demise.

The restaurant immediately hushed as the first strains of "O Lord of Space" echoed from our corner booth throughout the room. The rising and falling harmonies were almost haunting.

I finally opened my eyes again; a hundred more eyes were focused on us. We were surrounded by waitresses and bus boys.

The room exploded into applause before the male chorus barely finished their last G chord.

"That was just fabulously wonderful!" she gushed. "Sing another!"

And they began to sing "Without the Love."

I studied the faces of my men. There was Darrell, BMW and bird lover; Mark, Mario Lanza and Enrico Caruso lover; and Ed, Marilyn-and-only-Marilyn lover. But now as they fervently sang "Without the love of Jesus, my soul would die," I honestly believed them and began to wonder whether they were actually singing for the waitress or for all of heaven itself. You see, there was something special in their smiles and eyes.

But the thought quickly passed as our waitress began cooing compliments again. For this last song she had dragged out all the kitchen help, cashiers, and managers to listen. I felt on display, and the fact that I wasn't singing made me feel even more awkward.

Soon enough the show was over and we had explained to an elderly couple that no, we didn't know any Hank Williams's songs. Now we could finally eat. As usual, I'd been starved, but now I only glared at my French fries squirming in their blanket of catsup. My stomach was doing funny things.

I suppose everyone else enjoyed their meal—they looked disgustingly happy.

Too soon our waitress came bouncing back. Mirth-making rose to a crescendo again as our curly-haired heroine distributed a mailbag's worth of separate checks.

"I've certainly enjoyed being your waitress," she said, spreading the words like honey and smiling like a puppet.

I wondered whether she were vying for the largest tip in the history of Denny's, and was still deciding whether to scowl or

smile back, when she added, "And I won't let you
pray with me."

Suddenly the laughter died down, and she 
request, this time only softer. "Please pray with me.'

For a moment, the table was silent, then Pastor
"We'd be delighted. Won't you join us at the table?" He
motioned for her to sit down.

She glanced about the room and said, "I could get fired for
this," then proceeded to scoot in beside The Fellowship.

All was still as we bowed our heads, and Pastor Wick prayed
a simple prayer, asking the Lord to bless our waitress and to bless
our work.

There was silence for a moment longer, then the waitress
wiped her eyes and said, "Thank you."

And I wiped my eyes and said, "You're welcome."

♦ ♦ ♦

# Your Eyes Look Familiar

## *Rosarin Kriengprarthana*

I T'S a typical sizzling summer day in Bangkok. I try to cool
myself by fanning my face with a wilted magazine. It
doesn't work.

Fortunately, an occasional breeze wafts up from the
open windows of the stopped bus. The moving air half fans
me as I stand in the aisle.

I stare at a woman with a window seat. When the wind whips
through her black hair, I groan enviously. Why couldn't I be that
lucky?

*Come on, lady!* I plead silently. *Please get up so I can sit
down! I've had a hard day, and these stupid high heels are killing
me! I need a break!* Somehow I hope she'll read my mind. But she
tosses a haughty stare in my direction and turns away.

*Thanks a lot!* I fume.

Then I spot a vacant seat near the open door of the bus. "Aha!

᾿elief!" I mutter. Ignoring the looks of the other people on the bus, I sprint to the seat and plop down. Sighing, I close my eyes.

Minute after minute blissfully crawls by. I'm oblivious to my surroundings.

Suddenly a barrage of sound slams into me. My eyes spring open to investigate. The bus has stopped at the Klong Tuey Market, and an army of chattering people now push into the once peaceful bus.

One person catches my attention—an old, decrepit woman. She wears faded clothes frayed at the hems. And her hair, a shock of white, frames a face imprinted with lines of time. Lines that fan out and spread like cobwebs from her eyes, forehead, and mouth. The wrinkles seem to reveal that she's had a life of ceaseless worry and menial work.

But it's her expressive dark eyes that keep my attention riveted to her. They are eyes of intense pain.

I tear my gaze from her. I feel scared—scared of being sucked into her world, so different from my own safe cocoon. For the next few seconds I stare out the window without really seeing anything. The woman's image lingers.

All of a sudden the bus lurches, and a warm body is thrown against me. I reach out automatically to catch the figure. Slowly the person regains balance and straightens up. And I see it's *her*.

She looks at me with those unforgettable eyes. Then she speaks. "Thank you," she says.

"No problem," I reply, but I really want to scream at her, "What happened in your life to cause you such obvious pain? Tell me! I want to know!" My tongue thirsts to throw out questions. But I remain silent.

Then I see her wobble around on scarred and swollen feet as the bus driver hits the brakes. *Why doesn't somebody get up and let her sit down!* I pivot around in my seat, glaring from person to person. No one makes a move.

*I can't believe you all! You're not going to get up for her?* I cry silently. *Where is your compassion?*

*Where is* your *compassion?* a quiet voice asks from my brain. *What about the love that you, a Christian, should have for others?*

I recognize my conscience. But all the accumulated weariness in me explodes. I lash back in anger and rebellion. *Why should I always have to be the one sacrificing for others? I'm always walked on for being so nice! I'm tired too, you know. My feet are killing me, and it must be at least 100 degrees right now! I need to sit down!*

Silence. Then I hear another voice in my mind, with words I recognize from the Bible. *When, Lord, did we ever see you hungry or thirsty or a stranger or naked or sick or in prison, and we would not help you?*

A pause roars in my ears. Then I hear the reply. *"I tell you, whenever you refused to help one of these least important ones, you refused to help me."* *

I catapult out of the seat, my mind burning with those words. The old woman looks at me with confusion. But comprehension dawns on her, and she slumps into the seat.

Sweat streaks down her withered face, and she smiles. The beauty of that toothless and decayed grin radiates through me, and I feel cheap and ashamed.

"Thank you," she whispers.

I hesitate. "N-no problem." Quickly I turn away to hide the guilt in my eyes. And as the minutes tick by, I deliberately look everywhere except in her direction.

Then the bus slows to a stop, and people brush past me on their way out. And I know—I just *know*—that she has left the bus. For some strange reason I want to look at her one more time.

Staring out the window, I squint to catch a last glimpse of the lonely figure. She trudges up the street. Then her image begins to blur, and I begin to see, instead, a Man. Born and raised in a small town of Galilee. A Man who loved and gave, and in return received betrayal and death.

And I know without a doubt that the pain in that old woman's eyes could also be seen in that Man's eyes. As He hung on the cross dying, He knew all about it. And that pain is still in His eyes as He sees His hurting children, like this woman—and as He sees us betray Him day by day, minute by minute, when we pass Him by. He gives us chances every day to reach out to Him by helping others.

The bus hurtles on, leaving behind one old woman. And it takes with it a disciple who almost passed her Master by.

---

* Matthew 25:44, 45, TEV.

# FRIENDSHIP

*"A friend loves at all times"* (Proverbs 17:17, NIV).
*If that's the test of friendship, you'll experience some testing times with a cavern tour guide in "Whath Yo Name?" a student teacher in "Harry," a wild neighbor in "Joyriding."*

*There are also romantic friends, as in "Adoration" and "Three's a Crowd." Friends who play practical jokes. Friends of a different race. Childhood friends who grow up to meet again.*

*With true friends, there is no end . . .*

♦ ♦ ♦

# Whath Yo Name?

## *Carolyn Rathbun*

IT'S *going to be one of those hot sun-'n'-lizard days,* I mused to myself, *but I'll stay cool down in the cave.*

Tucking in a stray end of my blouse, I glanced at my colorful guide uniform reflected in the Moaning Cavern gift shop window.

I had never had such a delightful summer job, giving tours at this natural wonder and popular tourist attraction near Vallecito, California. Opening the door to the gift shop, I stepped in.

"Guess what, Carolyn," Deena greeted me, "your first tour this morning is a group of 25 mentally retarded adults on their way home from a week of camping. Good luck!"

I stopped in the doorway. "What? Wait a minute!" I said, but she hurried into the darkroom to develop a set of tour group photos.

It's not that I was prejudiced against mentally handicapped people, you understand. It's just that they are so strange and unpredictable to be around. In fact, the expression "mentally retarded" always reminded me of the time I walked through a psychiatric ward with my hospital administrator father and heard a patient screaming from her padded cell. The memory made me shudder.

*OK,* I told myself. *Let's think this through.* So far this summer, without too much stress, I had managed claustrophobic tourists, boisterous Boy Scout troops, and even a few squalling babies. But how would I ever get 25 uncoordinated, possibly dangerous, mentally handicapped adults down and then *back up* 236 steps on the cavern's see-through metal staircase?

I was getting scared. While I waited for the group to arrive I dusted around the cash register and rearranged merchandise on the gift shop shelves.

All too soon their white tour bus wound its way down the narrow road and into the gravel parking lot. Stepping out onto the porch, I surveyed the situation. The driver backed out of the door at the front of the bus.

*I'll bet he doesn't dare turn his back on them,* I thought nervously. *And I'm supposed to lead them down the staircase? Ha! I just hope no one is carrying a knife!*

"Now listen, everyone," the driver called from the bus's front door, "just keep your seats! Stay exactly where you are while I go buy the tickets."

I noticed several of the passengers, necks craned about, staring out the windows at me. Feeling mild revulsion, I avoided their gaze and forced a smile at the driver coming up the steps.

"Well, we made it!" he beamed. "Where do I get the tickets?" I pointed to the gift shop.

Soon he emerged and returned to the bus.

"All right, everyone, let's go see a cave!" he called jovially. The passengers, some of them struggling, rose from their seats and jostled into the aisle of the bus.

*Here we go,* I thought as they came off the bus, assisted by several chaperons. How perfectly they fitted my stereotyped mental image of what retarded people look like. Some walked with abrupt, twitching movements; others looked about them with vacant stares; one man was drooling; and a partially blind man in his 20s, lightly rocking his head back and forth, clung to the arm of a male chaperon.

I couldn't help feeling sorry for the group's escorts, locked into a demanding—even repulsive—responsibility like this. One of the chaperons, a gray-haired woman in her late 50s, smiled at me. Sympathetically I returned her smile, thinking how hard it must be to keep up a pleasant front in her position. How embarrassed she must feel, always having to be with this group of people!

Into the gift shop they came, smelling like the smoke from a week's worth of campfires. I tried not to breathe.

"This way, please," I announced, ushering them into the room housing the cave's original vertical drop, enclosed by a protective fence.

*I hope no one tries to jump the fence!*

"So glad you could all come out to the cave today." I smiled mechanically, feeling a twinge of guilt at my lie. "This is the cave's original entrance," I began my lecture, trying not to look at the man who was still drooling or at the young woman with mongoloid features who stood uncomfortably close to me.

During the first part of the presentation, I found myself focusing more and more on the faces of the chaperons, most of whom were middle-aged or elderly. I detected nothing except peaceful expressions, even when they were bumped by their constantly moving charges.

"Are there any questions?" I paused, silently planning my strategy to get this group down the spiral staircase.

"Yeth, I hab a questhion," lisped a slightly built Hispanic man with thick eyeglasses. Then he stopped and looked about with uncertainty.

"That's fine, Danny," the tall, graying bus driver reassured him. "Ask your question."

An eager grin spread across Danny's face as he again focused on me.

"Whath yo name?" he asked.

Smiling indulgently, I sighed. "My name is Carolyn. Now we are going to continue our tour down into the cave." Two women in the group who understood what I said giggled with childlike excitement.

Cautiously we made our way down to the upper platform in Moaning Cavern's Big Room, then down the spiral staircase.

I noticed how carefully, compassionately, the chaperons shepherded their motley group: encouraging clumsy Hilda, complimenting Bob on how well he was moving his legs, thanking

Nancy for not complaining on the long trip down. Funny, but I had never thought of this handicapped group as individual personalities who answered to their own names.

Although I no longer felt physically threatened by these visitors, I still found them unappealing. Again, I wondered about the patience of their escorts. Why would a person in his right mind give up life's normal adventures, slowing down to a little child's pace—intellectually as well as physically—in order to care for people such as these? It was beyond my understanding.

At the bottom of Moaning Cavern's Big Room, an expanse large enough to contain the Statue of Liberty, I launched into the last part of my lecture. I pointed out the 35-foot Igloo, the suspended Angel Wings, the MGM Lion, and other distinctive formations found in that roomy arena.

Although I had been here dozens of times, the serenity and grandeur of the highly decorated cave chamber never failed to overpower me and dwarf me as I looked into what resembled a vast crystal cathedral. It was with a twinge of reluctance that I brought every tour to an end.

"Are there any questions before we go back up the staircase?" I asked one final time.

"What's your name?" asked a stringy-haired, oversized woman in a flower-print dress. Where had I heard that question before?

"It's Carolyn," I answered, and a sponsor winked at me good-naturedly. "Any other questions? Yes, Danny."

"Whath yo name?" he asked, as he had at the beginning of the lecture.

"Danny," I answered, "you know what my name is. It's Carolyn." He smiled and nodded.

Just then the tall, nearly blind man, who had been clinging to his chaperon's arm ever since he'd entered the cave, released his hold and awkwardly pushed his way between Danny and the drooler. Walking unsteadily toward me, he stopped a few inches from my face. He leaned over, squinted into my eyes, and asked, "What's youw name?"

I could smell the outdoor aroma coming from his clothing. The entire group seemed taken aback and waited in silence for my answer.

I forced one last professional smile into his face and sighed, "Why, it's Carolyn."

He looked back at the others and gleefully repeated, "Why, it's Cawolyn." Then he added, "And she's nice."

Without warning, he suddenly turned toward me, threw his arms wide open, and gave me the biggest spontaneous bear hug I had had in a long time. Instinctively I returned his gesture with a quick squeeze. This unexpected encounter brought laughter from the group, and the drooler even applauded. I couldn't help laughing with them.

As the blind man's chaperon stepped forward and took his elbow, my prejudice against these gentle visitors evaporated.

"You're Carolyn," said the woman with mongoloid features, nodding approvingly during the trip back out of the cave. I returned her nod.

Both Bob and Nancy told me, "You're nice," when I assisted them on a few steps. Hilda reached out and lightly touched me as I passed her puffing heavily on her way up the stairs. Others smiled or stared in a comfortable, unaffected manner.

Suddenly I realized, with a bit of a start, that these handicapped people had accepted *me* as one of them. An hour before, this realization would have disgusted or frightened me. But now, for the first time since beginning work that morning, I felt good, very good.

Normally I said goodbye to my tour groups at the top of the cavern steps as we emerged into the gift shop. This time I found myself following them out the door and watching a bit wistfully as they boarded the bus.

Again I couldn't help noticing the courtesy with which the chaperons treated each individual as they saw the group members to their seats.

"You did very well in the cave!" announced the bus driver to the passengers, wiping his shiny forehead with a blue handkerchief. "Because you were so good," he continued with unflagging energy, "we are going to have a special picnic on the way home. How would you like that?"

Amid the group's approving chatter, he slid into the driver's seat, fastened his seat belt, and turned the key in the ignition.

Thoughtfully, I leaned over the railing of the front porch

while the bus turned around on the dusty gravel. I watched the vehicle lurch several times, gaining momentum as it turned back toward the parking lot entrance.

I spotted Nancy's cherubic face, and the blind man aimlessly moved his head about.

"Goodbye! Goodbye!" several began yelling.

" 'Bye now," the bus driver cheerfully called from his window as he drove past.

" 'Bye," I answered, feeling a sting in my eyes. I could see Danny's frantic wave.

"You're nisth," he called out, chin lifted above his half-closed window.

"So are you, Danny," I managed through a tight throat. "So are you."

◆ ◆ ◆

# Harry

## *Trudy J. Morgan*

I SWALLOWED hard, twice, as I climbed the steps of the school. I remembered the building well, but it had never seemed so silent as it did this morning on my first day as a student teacher. The kids were everywhere, talking to each other as loudly as ever, but nobody was talking to me. Even the ones who'd been there during my own days as a high school student gave me only corner-of-the-eye glances and corner-of-the-mouth hellos.

By lunchtime my worst suspicions were confirmed. Here, in my very own alma mater, I was as much a misfit as any student teacher anywhere was doomed to be.

I stood alone at the counter of the little store where most of the kids bought lunch. In the line behind me, I could hear Jeff and Danny talking. They were my last hope for any kind of enjoyment in my new situation. Now seniors, they had been freshmen my senior year here. We knew each other. I was about to turn around and say hi when I heard my name.

"Kate sure is stuck up now that she's a teacher," Jeff was saying. "She wants us to call her Miss Macgregor. As if I'd ever . . ."

I turned right around and stared him down. He faltered. "Oh . . . you're here," was all he could think of to say.

I didn't have enough pride left to march away with my head held high. I stayed behind and talked to him, and we patched it up.

The afternoon was just like the morning, only longer.

*I'm getting off to a great start,* I thought, falling into bed that night. The only bright spot on my horizon was that I wouldn't have to actually teach for another week.

Tuesday started off with as much promise as Monday. I'd given up wondering if I'd ever fit in. Now I was wondering if anyone would ever smile at me.

Second period was the only class I hadn't sat in on yet. This was the one I was supposed to start teaching next week. I was alert.

The kids filed into the classroom, and the ones I knew from outside school nodded at me. The last kid to walk in was one I'd never seen before—a skinny kid with a thatch of unruly brown hair and a wide grin. "Hi, Mrs. Johnston!" he bellowed at my supervising teacher. Then he noticed me cowering in the corner. "Hello, Miss Macgregor! Are you going to be our teacher?" I admitted I was, feeling better about the prospect already.

"That's Harry," Mrs. Johnston whispered to me.

The class was a rollicking 40-minute attempt to distract the teacher and avoid the study of English. My new acquaintance led in the fray. When it was all over, the kids made a break for the door. Harry paused and gave me his now-familiar grin. "Hope you enjoyed our class, miss," he said, then continued his mad dash for the door.

Later that day I waded downstairs through the between-class crowds. Harry caught my eye. "How are you surviving, Miss Macgregor?"

At that particular moment I was surviving pretty well.

Teaching Harry's class was fun. I began to get along with the other kids too. I started to fit in, to find a place of my own. It was beginning to be my school again, but in a different way.

Harry was still a bright spot in my day. One morning I was pinning cardboard across the windows so we could show a film. Harry came running into class, jumped a chair, shouted *"Look out, miss!"* and landed three inches from my unsuspecting back. Mrs. Johnston made him go back to the door and walk in properly.

We had a running joke, Harry and I. He always tried to get away with eating chocolate bars in class; I always tried to get them away from him. If I managed to get one, the whole class would applaud. If I wasn't fast enough, Harry would grin and offer me a piece of the bar as consolation prize.

The quarter began to move quickly. I was learning a lot about teaching, making a lot of mistakes, having fun. I enjoyed the students. I was getting along with most of them now.

Harry was still my favorite, but I became even more interested in him after one of our staff meetings.

Mr. Leffler leaned back in his chair. "I'd like to add another item to this agenda," he said. "There are some students who are . . . uh . . . doing rather poorly in their schoolwork and should really try to find . . . uh . . . another school for next year. Harry Wilson, for example. He's a fine young man, but—well, he's just not doing any work." Nods of approval from all the teachers. Other names were raised and discussed, but Harry was the one everyone agreed on.

I walked home feeling miserable. That good-for-nothing kid. Why am I so crazy about him? A smart-aleck kid from the wrong side of the tracks who listens to heavy metal music and comes to class reeking of cigarette smoke. And who doesn't do his school-work—which is the whole problem. What's he got going for him? A cute grin, a sense of humor, and a likable way with people. Those things might help him through life, but they won't get him through school. And they won't keep him away from the dangers in his own neighborhood. Things are bad enough now, and if he gets kicked out of school—where's he going to go?

*If I were a full-time teacher here,* I thought, *I'd fight for him. I'd make sure they gave him another chance, and then I'd make sure he did his work. I'd see he didn't get into any trouble . . .* The weight of my helplessness came down hard on my shoulders. I took my anger out on the pavement with fast, fierce steps.

That night it was hard to pray. One disarming grin kept

breaking through my other petitions. I tried to talk God into changing things.

"O God, please, please—he's such a good kid, God, but he could turn out so bad. Please look after him—take care of him. God, why do I beg You like this? You love him more than I do. You'll do everything You can for him, won't You? The trouble is, God, I'm afraid it won't be enough."

Two days later Harry breezed into class in a matching shirt and pants with a tie. Ties are an unknown species at our high school. I didn't remember ever having seen one on a student.

"Whoa!" I said.

"You like it, miss? I mean, you really like it?"

"It's great, Harry."

"No, seriously. Do you really seriously like it?"

"I really, seriously do."

All through class, while Harry and the others made valiant attempts to steer me off my subject, I wondered, *Has Mr. Leffler talked to Harry yet?*

They were all quiet now—as quiet as they ever got—working on their assignments. Harry, of course, was staring out the window.

"Miss Macgregor, I finally got it figured out why everyone hates school so much."

"Are you doing your assignment?"

"I will, miss. Just let me tell you this first. The reason everyone hates school so much is because of the principals. Just listen to this now, this is a little skit I got worked out in my head."

"Do your work, Harry."

"In a minute. You see, I go into Mr. Leffler's office—"

Finally I gave in and listened. This was interesting.

"I go in, and I see his collection. Have you seen his collection?"

I thought of Mr. Leffler's office, neatly decorated with diplomas and with pictures of his family. "What collection?"

"All over his office," Harry informed me with a gleam in his eye, "hangin' from the ceiling, he's got heads. Heads of students going way back to 1932. And he's sitting there with a loaded shotgun, and he shoves it up my nose and says, 'Harry, are you going to do better in your schoolwork?' And I know whichever way I answer he's going to pull the trigger. 'Cause this guy, he blows people away just for fun."

Somehow, I know not how, I steered the conversation into safer waters, like homework. That night I had another long talk with God.

"God, a kid like that deserves a chance. Even if he has to leave our school—at least look out for him. At least give him something good to hold on to. Show *me* if there's some way I can give him something."

I lay in bed, looking up beyond the ceiling at a God whose helplessness reflected my own. A God who loved all humanity, even a confused and bumbling student teacher, even more than I loved Harry. A God who had given everything good, only to find that sometimes it still wasn't enough.

The days sped by, gaining momentum as the end of the quarter drew near. I gave a test and Harry passed it—with a B, in fact. I knew from his joy that the experience was a rare one for him. I couldn't do a two-foot jump-kick right there in class as he did, but my heart was leaping. Other than that, things went on as usual. On the nerve-racking day when my university supervisor came to evaluate me, only one student stopped me in the hall to whisper, "How's it going, Miss Macgregor?" Harry might not always understand English literature, but he had an unerring instinct about people.

On the last day before I was to leave, the class was watching a film. Harry was out in the corridor helping Mr. Leffler with something when class started. I left the others and went out to retrieve him.

"Where's Harry?" I asked Mr. Leffler.

"Gone to find me a screwdriver. Oh—did the bell ring?"

"Yes. And we're watching a film. I don't want him to miss any of it."

"That's a sign of a good teacher. I'll go get him." Mr. Leffler disappeared into the janitor's closet and emerged with my lost sheep. We went into class.

When the bell rang again, the kids beat it out the door, same as always. I called Harry back.

"What is it, miss?"

I grinned, looking at him across the student-teacher gulf that lay between us. "I've never given you a detention, have I?"

"Oh, miss . . . I was helping Mr. Leffler. That's why I was late."

"Never mind, Harry, I'm just kidding. What I really wanted to say was—uh—thank you. I mean, you were a pain in the neck at times, but you've always been kind of . . ."

"Fun to get along with?" You had to hand it to the kid, he knew his strong points.

"Yeah, I guess so. It hasn't always been really easy for me, teaching here, but you've always been kind of friendly and you've made it a lot more fun for me." Then, to break the tension, I gave him a Mars bar. "I figured I owed you one, after all the stuff you gave me."

"Really? For me? You're serious?"

"Sure—only don't eat it in class!"

"How many times have I heard that! Thanks," he said, pocketing the bar.

We both turned to go out into the corridor. "Anyway," I said, "you're a real nice kid, so take care of yourself."

"You take care of yourself, too, miss."

Well, that was over. I went back to my classroom to wait out the last few class periods.

After school, as the kids were leaving, I heard a familiar voice outside the classroom door.

"Where's Miss Macgregor?"

"I'm in here. Come in," I called.

Harry made his entrance, knapsack slung over his shoulder. "I just came to say, miss, that it's been really enjoyable having you teaching here at our school." He shook my hand, one of those weird four-part handshakes that I can never get the hang of. We had one last good laugh as he taught me the moves.

"That's weird!" I said.

"It's my special handshake," he told me. "You can remember me by that," he added as he left.

I turned to put a book back in its place on the shelf. *Oh, kid,* I thought. *If that was all I had to remember you by, remembering would be very easy.*

♦ ♦ ♦

# Adoration

## K. Campbell Norskov

I'D never thought about Geoffrey until the day Debbie Pratt was in our dorm room describing the wonderfulness of their romance.

Cheryl and I were crouched around some white material on the floor. We continued to cut carefully around the pattern pieces while Debbie finished her account, including the embarrassing detail that Geoffrey used his protruding front tooth as an advantage. Then she mentioned that she was going to break up with him.

"What?" I exclaimed. "But you were just talking about wanting to sneak out with him!"

Debbie shrugged. "It's better to quit while you're ahead," she said, beaming a sophisticated smile down at Cheryl and me. "Gotta get," she announced abruptly, swinging her legs over the edge of the bed and starting for the door. "You oughta go for him, Sue," she called over her shoulder. "He's just your type."

The door slammed behind her, and my roommate collapsed on the floor, laughing.

"*Your* type!" Cheryl howled. "Everybody knows he's a druggie—and you're junior class pastor! What could you two have in common?"

I smiled.

"Why do we let Debbie in here anyway?" she muttered.

Cheryl crawled to her desk chair and sat down, opening her chemistry book. I leaned my head against the side of the bed and stared out the window, idly opening and closing my scissors. Geoffrey was a new senior from Oregon who played the guitar well, a pretty exotic combination for our small southern Christian school. I wondered if Debbie had seen some exotic streak in me that I'd missed.

Cheryl looked up sternly from her desk. "You don't really think he's your type, do you?" she asked.

I raised my eyebrows innocently. "Whatever would we have in common?" I asked.

"Oh, Sue!" Cheryl shook her head. "Sometimes I worry about you."

The next week Mr. Howard asked me to stay after band. I cleaned my flute while the band members swung their stands around and tramped out. I noticed that Geoffrey stayed too, draped over his seat at the end of our section, holding his flute lightly in his tanned hands.

"Sue," Mr. Howard said, stepping off his conductor's box, "you know Geoffrey, don't you?"

"Yes," I said, although I had never spoken to him. I smiled toward Geoffrey, who smiled obligingly just enough so that I glimpsed the famous tooth.

Mr. Howard plopped some music down on my stand and explained, "Geoffrey is doing exceptionally well in his flute lessons. I wondered if you would work up this piano accompaniment for our next tour. He'll probably be playing this solo at graduation, as well."

"Sure, Mr. Howard," I answered, picking up the music. I turned toward Geoffrey. "When's a good time for you to practice?"

He shrugged his shoulders and grinned. Here was a guy obviously shattered by Debbie's decision to stay ahead.

We started practicing the next day. I rushed to the music building after breakfast, but Geoffrey was already there, rolling off difficult tunes with a liquid tone. Maybe it was the tooth. I paused at the door and watched him slouching over the music stand, tapping his foot. After a few bars he looked up. I opened the door, and he lowered his flute.

"Hi," he said.

Geoffrey had a way with words.

The school year rolled past Christmas and into the early spring rites of band tours, class parties, and the student elections.

I was in the gym one afternoon tying a white sheet that read "Vote Sue Richardson, Religious Vice President" to the balcony railing when I heard liquid-clear notes float up from the gym floor, reverberating from the block walls.

Geoffrey was sitting cross-legged on a pile of tumbling mats, blowing into a wooden stick. In the empty gym the notes twisted and echoed as sweet as incense.

"Geoffrey!" I yelled. "What is that?"

His answer didn't carry, so I scurried down the stairs and loped across the empty basketball court to the mats.

"A recorder," he said.

By the end of the afternoon I talked him into letting me borrow his recorder. He had bought it in Belgium when his family had lived there. He got more exotic all the time.

I spent the next week improvising my own recorder descant to play along with one of Cheryl's tapes. I worked hard to get the recorder to sound pure and simple, and just a little lonely. I played it with my long hair out of its customary barrettes so that I would look the part of being on an Oregon beach at sunrise.

Cheryl remained uninspired.

"Sue," she interjected between my phrases one afternoon, "don't you think it's about time you took that thing back?"

The next evening at supper I marched boldly to where Geoffrey sat alone, and paused with my tray inches above the table.

"May I sit here?" I asked.

Geoffrey shrugged, "Sure."

I set the tray down and put the recorder between us on the table as I slid into the chair.

"I really like it," I said.

Geoffrey picked up the recorder, then put it back. "Keep it some more, then," he said.

Our romance had begun. The rest of supper was silent. Like I said, Geoffrey had a way with words.

I had read *Fascinating Girl*, and I knew that I should wait for him to initiate conversation. He did, once.

"What?" I asked, as quietly as possible.

He looked up from his tray, his eyes warm and brown. He shrugged, "Nothing."

After supper the next day Cheryl was waiting when I got back to the room.

"That's the second time that you've sat with Geoffrey at supper," she said. "What do you two have to talk about?"

I shrugged. "Music."

"Music," Cheryl muttered. "Sue, sometimes I worry about you."

Near the end of study hall Cheryl looked up from her chemistry book. "Have you wondered what God thinks about all this?" she asked.

"About what?" I asked.

Cheryl sighed. "About you and Geoffrey," she said.

"No," I answered.

A couple weeks later Geoffrey and I met in the woods for the first time. We climbed an old oak tree, and Geoffrey lay on his belly on a fat branch to watch a spider spin a web between a twig and a leaf.

"Geoffrey," I said, leaning against the trunk and rolling an acorn between my thumb and forefinger, "what do you think about God?"

"God," he repeated. He probably would have shrugged, but it would have imperiled his balance. "I sort of think that God is in everything—that spider, this tree." He paused. "You."

Suddenly I felt dizzy.

"I guess that means you'd call me a pantheist," he said.

I wouldn't have, because that was the first time I'd ever heard the word.

Cheryl pounced when I opened the door to our room.

"Sue," she said, "where have you been?"

"Geoffrey and I were talking," I said.

"Sue! You were out with Geoffrey?"

I shrugged. "We were talking about God."

I won the election despite my questionable companion—probably because my opponent had the unsavory reputation of never eating desserts. The results of the election were to be officially announced at the student association banquet.

After a flurried day of decorating the cafeteria and dressing for the banquet, I met Geoffrey at the side of the dorm, away from the main pack of students but close enough to hear the cellophane crackle and smell the florists' carnations.

"Here," he said when he saw me, and he gently crowned my unbarretted hair with a wreath he'd woven of daisies and Queen Anne's lace.

When I saw Cheryl's face as Geoffrey and I stepped through the Greek-ruin entranceway into the cafeteria, I knew I finally looked exotic. I tried to walk like a goddess.

After the banquet Cheryl was already in the room when I came in, my forehead burning from the kiss Geoffrey had brushed there.

Cheryl looked up at me as I drifted to the mirror to stare at the wreath.

"I don't know, Sue," she said. "Maybe he *is* your type."

My parents visited the next weekend. After a long Saturday lunch with Geoffrey, I walked them back to their car.

"Look, Sue," my father began, one foot already in the car, "you know we try not to interfere, but do you really think Geoffrey is your type? What sort of goals does this young man have?" He rapped the doorframe with his key. "What do you two have in common?"

Now hopelessly in love, I shrugged. "Music," I said.

April collapsed into May, and the seniors left on their trip. When he got back, Geoffrey seemed even quieter than before.

I knew it was over for us the night two of Geoffrey's friends joined us for supper. They talked loudly about the fun they'd had on their senior trip, while Geoffrey and I faced each other in silence.

Later, he confirmed it. We stood near a lamppost outside the gym, and I scratched circles in the gravel with my foot.

"Really, Sue," he said, "there's no use to plan on writing. I'm going back to Oregon. You've got to stay here."

His voice stopped.

Finally he finished, almost pleading. "You know. What do we have in common?"

I watched my shadow shrug and put my hands in my pockets. "Just music, I guess," I whispered.

I wanted to say something like "I had fun" or "I really like you" or "Thanks for teaching me the word *pantheism*," but I didn't.

"Time to go," Geoffrey said softly as the faculty patrol edged closer.

When I got to the sidewalk leading to my dorm, I turned to watch him move away, lean and silent as a cat.

Cheryl read my non-tear-marked face as soon as I walked in the room.

"Broke up with you, huh?" she said.

"It was mutual," I said, burying my head in my closet to sort my shoes. "We quit while we were ahead."

At graduation I sat in the front row of chairs in the gym with the rest of the junior class. On stage, Geoffrey rose for his solo, and I walked to the piano. He turned to me and nodded for the introduction, his robe sleeves billowing as he raised his flute. I played the beginning arpeggio, and his flute entered precisely, the notes falling as clean as pebbles into the silence.

When I sat down after the song, Cheryl leaned over.

"Good job, Sue," she whispered. Then she saw the music in my lap. Running her finger under the title, she said, " 'Adoration.' That was a good song for you two."

I twisted my mouth into a smile and stared at the music until it blurred.

♦ ♦ ♦

# Rope Pull

## Charles Wilkinson

THIS was no ordinary tug-of-war. The Walla Walla High School faculty-student pull was held with the rope stretched across the small creek that meandered through campus. And the event was always held at a special time: the first Monday after ice formed on the creek.

I had been asked to join the faculty team. Although still technically a college student, I was doing my student teaching at "Wa-Hi," as it was called. The students in my homeroom, 5-24, told me that being asked to be on the 20-man faculty team was a great honor, and that I would lose face if I didn't join. I wasn't so sure, but it sounded like fun, so I agreed.

The first ice on the creek was spotted early one week, giving everyone plenty of time to plan. The students put a lot of effort into preparing for the event, even staging trial pulls to select the 20 strongest boys. Then with great pomp, their team announced that they had all sworn to go into the water. Usually, after the first few people had been pulled to the water's edge, everyone let go. But this year's student team was determined that, even if pulled clear into the water, they would hang on, take advantage of the hill on the opposite side, and pull us back down into the creek with them. Rumor had it that one boy was bringing a wet suit.

The leader of the faculty team was quick to announce, without consulting us, that we had taken the same vow. But the faculty announcement seemed a bit "me too," and it was clear that the students had the psychological advantage. The teachers made plans to bring an extra change of clothes that day, but our hearts were not in it.

Friday we had a pep rally in the gym. Seniors, juniors, and sophomores (there were no freshmen), seated on separate bleachers, whooped it up with cheers for their class. Then all 1,800 of them yelled at once. It was deafening! The rally was mainly a buildup for the weekend's football game, but the tug-of-war teams were also introduced—the student team to roars of applause, our team to weak cheers from the faculty section.

When Monday morning arrived, the students suspected that we were up to something when the vice principal summoned the faculty team to his office before classes. The students called the vice principal "Worm-lip" because he generally held his mouth in a tightly compressed manner. He was an exceptional disciplinarian, and was disliked, yet respected, by the students.

At the midmorning break the student team quickly got dressed in old jeans, T-shirts, and old shoes, but no wet suits. The faculty team headed to the lounge to change, except we changed nothing but our shoes. The loose-jawed boys stared as we strode out wearing slacks, dress shirts, and ties. Several men even had coats on, and Worm-lip was in a three-piece suit. "We didn't bother to change because we're not going into the water," Worm-lip said coldly. "You are!"

Someone on the student team shouted "Let's get 'em!" and both sides of the creek came alive with whistles and cheers. The PE coach handed the rope down to both sides, someone blew a whistle, and we were off.

The initial pull found us moving closer to the water. It was obvious from the roar of the crowd that the favored team was winning. We were dragged to a point where two of the teachers had their feet in the water. I looked at the cold water, thought about Worm-lip and his big mouth, and then about my good slacks, and suddenly I was mad. I started pulling harder on the rope. The same psychology must have been working on the others, because just then the rope stopped moving.

For a moment we were absolutely motionless, and the campus fell quiet, except for a splashing sound as the two teachers in front repositioned their feet in the mud under the water. Finally the whole procession started moving back our way, slowly at first, then gaining speed until we had to scramble up the bank. The student team hit the water so hard that several of them went clear under headfirst. They all let go, and we dragged the rope out on our side before stopping to catch our breath. The whole student team was standing knee-deep in the water staring at us, and there was an awkward silence. Someone muttered, "The big bullies won!" and the girls cooed a sympathetic "Awww!"

But one of the students in the creek wasn't going to let it end that way. "They beat us!" he shouted. "They beat the best! Let's hear it for the old men!"

The cheering and clapping started with the students in the creek and spread to the whole crowd. Suddenly we were all friends again. We wrapped the students in the blankets we had brought for ourselves, and shared a lot of good humor and congratulations. Someone even slapped Worm-lip on the back—with a wet hand. Finally I headed back to U.S. History, where I discovered I was incapable of picking up a piece of chalk.

Today, the only physical reminder I have of my student teaching at Wa-Hi is a bronze-apple trophy from my 5-24 homeroom group. But my warmest memory is of the sportsmanship of a beaten tug-of-war team. In a few seconds they changed the mood of the whole school. It was more than sportsmanship. It was a Class Act.

♦ ♦ ♦

# Joyriding

*Dolores Klinsky Walker*

**M**OM told me it was a mistake to spend so much time with Susie that I didn't make other close friends, but I figured, what did she know? The summer Susie moved away I found out.

I knew kids from school and church, but *acquaintances* and friends to hang out with are two different things. It was too much, I knew, to expect a copy of Susie to move into her former house, but when I finally saw a leggy blonde my age in the yard next door, my heart took the elevator up. My mother had all the facts on the new family before I got home from babysitting that afternoon.

"Mrs. Gorand said they moved out here to get away from some 'undesirable elements'—whatever that implies," Mom informed me with an appraising look. "The girl doesn't seem like your type, but she *is* a newcomer. It can't hurt to be friendly."

That's once Mom was wrong.

Lynne definitely wasn't my type. For starters, she wasn't timid like I am. She knocked on our door that evening, wearing skimpy pink shorts and a halter, with a half-smoked cigarette dangling from her fingers. I steered her to the patio instead of asking her in.

*She knocked on the wrong door,* I thought to myself as she propped her legs up on the patio table. Dorene—who lives at the end of our block—was a match for her. Susie and I had enjoyed only a nodding acquaintance with Dorene, but every time she ran away from home her mother called our mothers to ask if we'd seen her.

At least I didn't have to worry about what to say with Lynne. She talked nonstop, mostly about recording stars. I wasn't sorry when Mom called me in.

Later, though, I softened toward Lynne. Obviously she was lonely too. Maybe we could find a common interest and do something together at school. Susie and I had talked about working on the school paper. I mentioned it to Lynne.

"Are you crazy?" she exploded. "Write something I don't *have* to?"

"Maybe you could be a photographer . . ." I could tell I wasn't convincing her.

She stabbed a cigarette into the grass. "School isn't where the action is, Tammy." A calculating look stole into her eyes. "Or maybe it is. I'll ask Dorene."

So they had met without my help. They would be nothing but trouble for each other, I knew. It would be hard to offset Dorene's bad influence on Lynne, but I was determined to try. At least I'd hang in there and be a friend as long as Lynne would let me.

Then Mom switched sides. "I really wish you'd try to find some other friends," she said. "Every time you come from Lynne's, you smell like a walking ashtray."

"But I've got to be her friend if I'm going to influence her for good!" I shouted.

"Tamara Mae Wahlstrom," Mom responded, leaving a weighty pause between the words, "I'll thank you not to shout at me. That may be OK next door, but not here. It appears Lynne is influencing you, not the other way around."

Her words stung, but she had a point. Lynne *was* influencing me. For instance, she had this idea that everybody was out to get her. Unreasonable adults forced her to go to school. An unjust judge gave her mother custody after the divorce and ordered her father to stay away. She even took it personally when her record club's computer billed her twice for the same record. Now she had me wondering if some malevolent force had moved Susie away just to make me miserable.

But I liked going next door where a teenager ruled for a change. Sprawling on Lynne's unmade bed and listening to Dorene and Lynne talk above the blaring stereo wasn't my idea of fun, but it beat sitting alone in my room.

And I *could* say no when it mattered. Like when they tried to share a joint with me sometimes. I always passed it on. Once Susie and I had tried sniffing something that was supposed to get us high and I didn't like the feeling of being out of control. I tried to tell Lynne and Dorene that was why I didn't mess with drugs.

"But being out of control's where it's at!" Lynne had responded.

Dorene laughed and added, "I'll bet she won't even ride a roller coaster! No brakes!"

Right.

We had become a strange threesome, thrown together by proximity and loneliness. I tried to pray for Dorene and Lynne, but if God was doing anything in their lives, it wasn't noticeable. I wanted to ask them to youth events at church, but I never mustered the nerve. I don't know which prospect shook me more—their scornful laughter at my invitation, or the thought of walking through the church doors accompanied by two smoky strangers with wild hair.

But determined to exert a positive influence, no matter how small, I suggested we go bowling one night. That's such "good clean fun," I was surprised they agreed.

"My mom will take us," Lynne volunteered quickly. "Yours will bring us home, won't she, Dorene?" A silent message passed between them.

Dorene nodded.

We had a good time at the bowling alley. In addition to bowling, I saw some classmates from school and discovered I was looking forward to school starting. Living in Lynne and Dorene's never-never land had begun to wear on me.

When we left the bowling alley, Dorene's mother was nowhere in sight. Lynne and Dorene prowled the parking lot while I stood by the curb, watching for her mother's beat-up Chrysler. Suddenly Lynne yelped, and I went over to see what was up.

"Found one!" She waved a set of car keys at us, then slid behind the wheel of a dirty old station wagon. "Some nice person must have known we'd need a way home." I backed away, but Dorene blocked me. "Come on, don't be a wimp!"

I refused to move. "I'll wait for your mother."

Dorene laughed. "You'd wait forever." She opened a car door and gave me a shove that threw me onto the seat, then jumped in behind me and slammed the door. Lynne coaxed the engine into starting. The terror I had felt before my first roller coaster ride was nothing compared to this.

"Do you even know how to drive?" I sputtered.

"What do you think I did time—" Lynne broke off abruptly as the ignition caught.

I considered wrestling the steering wheel from her, but what if we lost control and hit another car? For once I wished I were more like my companions. They didn't know the meaning of the word consequence.

My fingers dug into the dashboard as we lurched out of the parking lot. Lynne turned right—not left toward home.

"How about a little ride in the country?" Lynne laughed as she pushed the gas pedal to the floor.

I glanced at the speedometer and then noticed the gas gauge. "If we go very f-far," I stammered, unable to control my fear, "we'll have a long walk back."

Dorene gave me a dirty look. "It's on empty," Lynne admitted. She reversed our general direction by careening around the block. Lynne paid no attention to speed limits or stop signs, so I expected the wail of a siren at any moment. I *hoped* for that sound, but it never came.

We were approaching a shopping center with gas stations.

"Lynne, please stop! I have to go to the bathroom," I ventured.

Dorene elbowed my ribs. "That's *too bad.*" Lynne passed a gas station without letting up on the accelerator. At least we were heading toward our side of town.

"Nobody's seen us, right? No way to trace the car to us?" Lynne shouted across me to Dorene.

"Unless Tammy here talks." Dorene jabbed me again.

Lynne glanced over and smiled. "She's never gone joyriding before. Maybe it's scary the first time. I can't remember."

Dorene found that hilarious. After she stopped laughing, she turned to me without a trace of warmth. "You'd better not tell. You're an *accomplice.* If we get in trouble, *you* get in trouble, understand?"

Two blocks from home Lynne pulled over to an unlighted curb. She shut off the engine, patted the dusty dash, then rubbed away the finger marks. "Thank you for a nice ride home, car."

Lynne and Dorene linked arms and giggled as they skipped down the street. But my steps dragged. I couldn't tell my parents what had happened, and I didn't want to start lying. What would I say?

Lynne and Dorene walked me to the door and rang the bell before I could get inside. When Dad opened it, Lynne said, "Maybe you can cheer up Tammy. Her score was lousy."

Dad looked surprised, but he let me pass without comment.

"Did you have fun, dear?" Mom asked, but I walked straight to my room without replying.

The next day Mom and I went shopping for school clothes. She suggested we take Lynne. "It might help her get excited about school," she said. I vetoed the idea immediately. Mom looked puzzled, but she didn't push it.

It was easy to pretend Dorene didn't exist, but Lynne was another matter. She was baffled that I held a grudge—which is how she saw it. "I thought we were *friends,*" she pouted.

I looked at her—frizzed blonde hair, muddy-blue eyes, a turned-up nose that had once seemed saucy and cute. She waited impatiently for my response. I searched for something that could possibly convey my conflicting thoughts.

"I'd like to be your friend," I said at last. "But we live in two different worlds. I don't belong in yours, and you aren't comfortable in mine." I had a picture in my mind, but it wasn't easy to transfer into words. "Maybe now and then we can meet on the bridge between, OK?"

Lynne just shrugged and walked away. I'm not sure she understood my answer. But I gave her all I could afford to give.

◆ ◆ ◆

# Playing Good Samaritan
## *Gina Lee*

I MET Dave at a speech contest in a far-off city. He was surrounded by a crowd of admirers oohing and ahing over his guide dog. I suppose that inside they were really marveling at the sureness and agility of a blind person.

When I saw him I wanted to meet him because—well, frankly, because I was curious. I had known old people before who were blind, but never a guy my own age who was blind. I wondered how he managed extracurricular activities, let alone school itself. But I was too scared to go up to him and introduce myself, so I sat in a miserable heap on a cold step.

The final round of the speech contest began, and the crowd gradually dispersed to go listen to the speeches. It was then that Dave, a fellow loser, came over and introduced himself to me.

"Hi. What was your speech about?" he asked.

The question surprised me. How did he know I wasn't a teacher?

"Tolerance," I answered.

"Oh. I gave mine on the 18-year-old voter. I guess we both bombed out."

"I guess so."

"Did you make it to the semis?"

"No. Did you?"

"No."

We sat there on the step in silence for a while. My feet were freezing in the brisk wind. I was just wishing I had worn some warmer shoes instead of my flimsy sandals when Dave persuaded his big German shepherd to lay down on my feet. The dog was heavy and shedding fur all over the place, but after that my feet were warm and cozy.

Dave and I whiled away the long hours talking about nearly everything under the sun, and I found to my surprise that he was quite a guy.

The trouble began when Dave suggested going to the student snack shop for some hot cocoa. As luck would have it, when we sat down at a table to order, I saw some of my friends come in the door.

"Hey, who's your friend?" Ralph asked.

"This is Dave," I answered. "Dave, the guy I'm talking to is Ralph. He's got his girlfriend Amber with him, and Peggy's right behind him."

Peggy made a face at my awkward introductions, but it was Amber who dropped the bomb. She got a sarcastic grin on her face and I knew that she was going to say something awful—and she did.

"Playing good Samaritan?"

Ralph coughed loudly, and Dave just sat there pretending he hadn't been insulted.

Peggy smiled nervously and said, "Well, I guess we'd better go. Nice to meet you. Come on, Amber." Peggy managed to ease Amber out the door before she had time to say anything worse.

But Ralph was still standing there—sweet, kind Ralph that I had known since the first grade. "Hey man, she didn't mean anything by that remark," he said awkwardly.

"That's OK. Forget it," Dave said.

"Well, ah, be seein' ya. I mean, I hope I can. . . . It was nice meeting you." Ralph rushed out the door as fast as possible without breaking into a run.

I was still sitting there, not knowing what to do, when Dave broke the silence. "Hey, do you still want that cocoa?"

"Sure."

We passed a wonderful day together, talking and just enjoying the company. I discovered that Dave had set some high goals for himself, including becoming a lawyer. I didn't make any of the mistakes you always hear of sighted people making—like carefully avoiding the word "see," even when it crops up naturally in the conversation.

All too soon the day was over. The beautiful trophies were given out to the deserving winners. Everybody started to leave the hall where the awards had been given out, and Dave fastened his dog into her harness, said his goodbyes in a hurry, and then left to avoid the crowd.

On the bus on the way home, Peggy sought me out. "I just wanted to tell you how sorry we all feel about what Amber said in the snack shop. I think it was real nice of you to hang around with that blind guy. I wish I'd thought of it myself."

"I wasn't—" My voice was louder than I had intended it to be, and I calmed down a bit before beginning over again. "I wasn't hanging around him to be nice to him."

"You weren't?" Peg was honestly surprised.

"No, I wasn't. I was hanging around with him because I was interested in him."

"Romantically interested?"

"That's right."

"Yeah. Well, you know the old saying, 'To each her own.' "

" 'To each her own,' " I echoed, and she laughed and moved back to her own seat.

Then it was Ralph's turn. He crawled on his hands and knees clear from the back of the bus just to straighten things out.

"I'm really sorry about Amber," he told me. "I don't know why she'd say a dumb thing like that."

"It's OK," I said quietly. "You don't have to apologize for her. It's over. Just forget about it."

"OK." Ralph's face broke into a relieved grin. "Glad you feel that way. I gotta go back now before the driver sees me crawling around."

I saw Ralph and Amber and Peggy often at school after that, but I never heard from Dave again. I guess 10 years from now I'll be wondering whether Dave really liked me or whether he was just being kind to a lonely girl.

◆ ◆ ◆

# Black Lace

## *Cathy Parker McBride*

ATLANTA, Georgia, 1953. I stood at the bus stop wrapped in twirling, spinning snow. Sweet stuff. Soft stuff, like peeking out at the world through lace curtains. Snow's not a familiar friend to us Georgians.

When the driver honked, the impatient mob bumped me toward the bus. I felt like a baby getting a whipping through the thick diaper of my winter coat.

When I finally made it on the bus, I looked around for an empty seat, hoping. I didn't see any—except one near the back of the bus. A tall Colored girl sat next to it.

More people pushed in behind me, and they scooted me down the aisle. Before I knew it I was shoved right up against that empty seat.

Mustard. Soured milk. Cheap wine. That's what the bus

smelled like. The fat man sandwiched in behind me kept puffing hot, sticky air down my neck and punching me with his metal lunch box. I wondered how long it'd been since his last bath. The Camel cigarette advertisement above me got fuzzy, and I steadied myself on the back of the empty seat . . . Then I heard her.

"Sit down, sister," she said. Her voice sounded crisp but faraway, like a wind chime on a breezy day.

I glanced down and managed a limp smile. "That's OK. I'm all right," I lied. Then I quickly added, "Thank you, though." After all, Mama always taught me to be kind to Coloreds.

To tell you the truth, I wanted to ooze into that floor, I felt so nauseated. But a White couldn't sit in the back of the bus with a Colored. It just wasn't done. Not in 1953. And why did she call me "sister"? I'd never heard a Colored call a White "sister," or vice versa.

About that time the bus jerked to the left, and without trying, I flopped into that empty seat. It felt so-o-o good. I couldn't have moved if I'd wanted to. Anyway, I reasoned, what would it hurt? There were Whites one seat ahead.

For maybe five minutes, we just sat there, Sahara and I, silent as shadows. I remember the sound of the Coloreds laughing and joking behind me. Up ahead, the Whites were solemn as midnight clocks, nobody talking.

"Well, how does it feel, sister?" she finally asked.

I turned to face her, and her beauty startled me. Skin as lush as black roses. Eyes, mysterious, like two oceans. Elegant.

"What?" I asked, jerking my mind back to reality.

"I said how does it feel, sister? To be sittin' next to a Colored?"

What did she want me to say? In all honesty it didn't feel like anything unusual, but I couldn't say that.

"Why do you call me that?" I asked.

"Call you what?" She smiled slyly. She knew what I meant.

"Sist . . ." I started. "Sister," I managed.

She didn't blink. "Because someday we will be." Then she turned toward the window and studied the spinning snow. *What did she mean someday we'd be sisters?*

"How much longer is your bus ride?" I asked, feeling uneasy with the silence.

"It takes me an hour to get to school," she answered.

"What school?" I asked.

"My dancin' school."

"You're a dancer?" I asked with wide eyes. Not many people danced where I came from in south Georgia. Like my preacher daddy always said, "dancin's a tool of the devil."

"Ballet," she answered. "I've been takin' ballet for 14 years."

I didn't know much about ballet. But at least it was respectable.

"I'm a writer," I said. "Today'll be my first day in graduate school."

She studied me for a while, then gave me a smile that was wise and deep and knowing.

"Do you know why you write, sister?" she asked.

Her words stung my mind, then swarmed about me, hesitant to land. No one had ever asked me that before.

"Well, sure," I stalled. "Of course I know. It's just . . . well, you'd think I was silly."

Her look was a dare.

"Well . . . it's like . . . ," I hesitated, wondering if I could trust her. "Well, to tell you the truth, it's sort of like when I write I feel like my soul's being set free. Like thoughts are prisoners, and only I can give 'em freedom."

Suddenly, I felt as naked as a shelless turtle. I'd never talked like that to anybody before, especially a stranger, especially a Colored stranger.

"Why do you dance?" I blurted out.

She sighed and brushed her fingers through the side of her dark hair. "My friends say Sahara's a crazy dreamer," she said. "You see, sister, I keep thinkin' that through my dancin' I can add something special to people's lives. Maybe even help people understand God's grace a little better." She laughed a quick little laugh and shook her head. "I don't know. Lately I've been thinkin' of givin' it up."

"Why?" I asked. I thought how it'd feel to give up my writing. It would be like having my heart ripped right out of my chest.

"Maybe I am a crazy dreamer. Maybe I'm finally facin' the fact that I'll never really touch people with my dancin'. What chance does a Colored have to make a difference, anyway?" She got a faraway look in her eyes, like she was talking to somebody I could never know. "When I dance," she continued, "people clap, but not with their souls. I want to touch people's souls, sister; do you know what I mean?"

I knew what she meant. I felt the same way about my writing.

"I'll probably never give it up, though," she sighed. "After all, it takes time to grow a rose. That's what Mama's always tellin' me, anyhow."

All that day, thoughts of Sahara haunted me.

Anyway, the next day, I was pleased to see her ballet slippers lying on the seat beside her. Empty places next to Whites stared at me. But I walked to the back of the bus. "Is . . . is this seat taken?" The words came out cracked and bruised, but when they were out, it felt right.

Our friendship continued like that for more than a month. Every day, there'd be Sahara's worn ballet slippers, and I'd settle in next to her. For an hour going and an hour coming home, our words flowed like summer rain. Our cultures were as different as air and water, but our souls were identical twins.

"I want to see you dance," I yelled to Sahara one morning over the roar of the bus. "I've been thinkin' it over and I want to go to your recital next week."

Sahara's brow crinkled with concern. "I don't think you should," she said weakly. "The place . . . I might disappoint you, sister."

"No," I argued. "You've read my stories; now I want to see you dance. I'm coming next week . . ."

Forgive me, but that first time I saw Sahara's school, I felt like my soul had been defiled. I just couldn't stop crying. Peeling paint, drooping gutters, garbage-lined streets, and a performance hall hardly large enough for a busy mouse. A decaying log, that's what that old place reminded me of. Beautiful Sahara—it just didn't seem right. But then she started dancing . . . and nothing else mattered.

You'd have to create new words to describe Sahara that night. All I can say is she looked like some fine bird soaring in a summer sun. Every leap and whirl throbbed with so much power she took my breath away. And her grace almost drowned me.

When the music stopped, nobody moved. We just sat there, wrapped in some sweet womb of warmth. Finally somebody on the front row started to applaud. Slowly at first, as if each clap were deliberate, almost painful. Then another applauded and another, until the explosion of clapping souls blinded me. And our tears also were our applause.

For maybe five minutes, clapping tore through that hall like thunder. We couldn't stop. The Colored lady next to me leaned over and hollered something in my ear, but I ignored her. I needed to be alone with Sahara's victory. I wanted to believe my writing could touch people too. But the old woman wouldn't give up.

"Have you ever seen anything like that child?" she yelled. "She makes me think of . . . I don't know. Lace maybe. Yeah, that child makes me think of a piece of fine black lace."

"Black lace?" Her words confused me. They sounded nice, but peculiar, too. Black lace. Black lace. My mind caressed the words, trying to understand their meaning. Lace.

I studied Sahara as her arms swept high above her sleek body and then floated to the floor in a final bow. *She is like lace,* I thought. Black lace. But why do the words sound so strange, so unfamiliar? Then a thought forgotten flowed over me, and I looked at Sahara with new eyes. *Black,* I thought. Black.

My sister is black.

♦ ♦ ♦

# Three's a Crowd

*Gary L. Bradshaw*

BORN the son of an itinerant worker, I spent my childhood as the world's "new kid." And now, in high school, I was the new kid again.

To make matters worse, I was experiencing that first fearful attack of the kind of love that drives men and boys to commit unexplainable actions in its name. A love unrequited.

Winter had set in. And by this time the school was buzzing about another new kid in town named Jim. He was from the north, a yankee. His father, the new band instructor, was a strict disciplinarian and not too popular.

Jim was unlike anyone we had ever known. Blond-haired and blue-eyed, he had a quick wit and a quicker laugh. His slick wardrobe included white shirts, ties, cashmere sweaters, and a fancy leather coat. Residents of our cow town usually wore faded blue jeans, plaid shirts, cowboy boots, blue jean jackets, and wooly underwear.

Jim mesmerized the teachers and the girls. But his appearance and mannerisms irritated the boys. They disliked him, believing that he thought himself better than they.

Somehow Jim and I became friends—maybe because we were the two newest students around. And as our friendship grew, his home became my second home. It was like none I had ever seen. No television. Books everywhere. (And Jim seemed to have read them all.) Instruments, songbooks, and records. His family of five sang and played together. And they talked—all the time.

They were Jehovah's Witnesses. At that time I couldn't comprehend religious bigotry, but I heard the comments of the people concerning their faith. The small town's dislike for Jim's family puzzled me.

I didn't ask Jim what a Jehovah's Witness is because I didn't consider it a necessary thing to know. But he did like to talk about God, and he knew how to make me think about what he was saying.

Jim called me his buddy. "Buddies," he explained, "are people of the same heart, the same spirit, who place the cares and feelings of the other above their own." We shared our visions, our sadness, our joys, and our love for the good things in life.

Then there was this girl.

She was one of those we've all known: hypnotic eyes, dimples, and just a sprinkling of freckles across the nose. She flitted from guy to guy, leaving a trail of shattered self-images in her wake. Not seeing her as poison to my ego, I worshiped her from afar.

Actually she lived right down the street from me, alongside the sawmill that her father owned. Her nearness at night sometimes kept me awake. Then every morning on my way to school and every evening on my way home I trailed far behind her as we walked the railroad tracks into town. She was never alone. Beside her walked her latest beau.

Then one day luck smiled on me. This girl decided that I would be her next victim. Leaving the other boys, she walked with me. She smiled, and my brain melted. She began to talk, and my heart palpitated. My temples were about to explode. I tried to speak, but only squeaked. My knees wobbled, my throat felt parched, my stomach churned. Then I stubbed my toe on a railroad tie.

Despite such an unpromising beginning, we were holding hands by the third day. This tempestuous love affair lasted for two weeks, during which time she, Jim, and I were together constantly—my two best friends.

Then I began to sense an imbalance of friendliness taking shape. To put it bluntly, Jim was becoming more friendly with her. But caring for them both, I shrugged it off.

They didn't have the courage to tell me. The school newsletter lay on my desk. It contained a nasty gossip column, and my name was in print for the first time. "HEY, GARY," it read, "DID YOUR BUDDY JIM STEAL JANICE AWAY FROM YOU?"

Later that day I was informed they had been seen pressing their lips together at a ball game. My dreams of an early marriage and a trip to Europe followed by years of nuptial bliss wafted away in a puff of smoke.

I was not kind to Jim that day. He tried to talk to me, but I wouldn't listen. When the final bell rang for the day, I raced home so I didn't have to see either of them.

At home I energetically offered my father help at his gas station. He was stunned. Dust flew as I swept floors. Soap flew as I washed windshields. Sweat flew as I raced from car to car, feverishly attending to the rush of late afternoon traffic.

I had exerted myself for the better part of an hour and was in the process of filling up a car for a man who wanted only $2 worth. Then the sound of footsteps came from behind me. I turned around.

Jim stood two feet away—well within punching distance. Seeing the barbaric look on my face, he raised his hands, palms out.

"Gary, you have every right to punch me out if you want to," he pleaded, "but I have something to say first. Then if you want to hit me . . . it's OK."

My anger didn't go away instantly. But it did as he told me that our friendship was more important to him than any girl could ever be. "If it means that we can't be friends because of her . . . if our friendship would be over . . . then she's history as far as I'm concerned."

Now I was stunned.

Jim threw his arm around my neck, and we walked off, leaving the gas pumping.

We headed straight for her house. I had decided if I was important enough to Jim for him to give her up, then he was important enough to me to give her to him. And I wanted to tell her she didn't have to sneak to see Jim anymore.

As it went, their love didn't last long. But you know, my friendship with Jim did, to this day and beyond.

◆ ◆ ◆

# K. Ruth Was Here

*Shelly Peters*

IT was Saturday night, and the official Saturday night activity was terrifically boring. As the inactivity progressed, Erin and I decided we would sneak back to the dorm to listen to my illegal radio. Arriving at my room, I lifted the pillow under which I had stashed my radio earlier that evening.

"Uh-oh!" I choked to Erin. For there in place of my radio was a yellow slip of paper bearing the dreaded and all-too-familiar message "K. Ruth was here." The dean, K. Ruth, had found and confiscated my radio.

"I'm getting sick of this!" I fumed. "How come she always searches my room? I'm in the mood for revenge." I stopped suddenly, my scheming mind kicking into action.

"Hand me the knife, Erin," I whispered, though everyone should have been long out of earshot.

With Erin's help I quickly picked the lock on the door to the dean's apartment. We headed straight for the dean's bed, hurriedly disassembled it, and transported it to the dorm basement. Then came the final touch. In the center of the floor where the bed had been we strategically placed a yellow slip bearing the message "S. Elizabeth was here."

Pleased and somewhat awed with our deed, we headed back to my room to wait for K. Ruth.

When the dean finally did burst into my room she was furious, but she tried to stay calm as she commanded Erin and me to return her bed "this instant."

Boldly I shot back, "I hope you are really mad, 'cause I sure am! How come you always search my room and—?"

That did it. K. Ruth let loose with all her fury. We yelled back and forth, I hurling insults as fast and thick as I could, and she coming right back at me with a few choice comments of her own. All the while Erin and I were walking toward the basement to return K. Ruth's bed as commanded.

The next day the whole thing seemed like a bad dream. Had I really said all those stinging words to the dean? I looked down at the yellow slip on the floor. My mind raced ahead: I had been suspended once already and had been told that one more problem would likely send me home for good. The administrative committee surely wouldn't hesitate to boot me when they heard about this.

Monday morning I was called in to plead my case before the ad committee. There sat K. Ruth at the end of the table. She seemed quietly determined. When they were through questioning me I walked back to the dorm to await the final decision. I also got out my suitcases and started packing.

All too soon I was called into the principal's office. The principal glared at me before he spoke, "You will be suspended for two weeks for continued insubordination. If you so much as *blink your eyes wrong* you won't graduate. You understand?"

I nodded, too shocked to say a word. I was staying. Then he shocked me even more. "The only reason you're being allowed to come back," he continued, "is because your dean persuaded the committee to let you stay."

K. Ruth had fought for me in ad committee! Why?

Two months later I was standing in the middle of campus, my

graduation gown glistening in the sun. A tassel tickled my ear, gold cords hung around my neck, a fresh diploma and scholarship award rested in my hand. I spotted K. Ruth in the crowd, and moments later I was hugging her goodbye.

"You know," I said, "I think I'm actually going to miss you, K. Ruth."

K. Ruth smiled. "I think I'm actually going to miss you too, S. Elizabeth."

"There's something I want to show you, because I know this is the only reason I'm here today." I handed her my diploma binder. "Go ahead," I urged, "open it up."

She slowly opened the binder, and I watched her eyes fill with tears. For there in the middle of the diploma hung a faded yellow paper bearing the message "K. Ruth was here."

♦ ♦ ♦

# One More Play

## *Christopher V. Cassano*

HEY, man," he says, "we gotta play ball sometime." He looks the same, maybe a few pounds heavier, but still the same.

*(Has it really been five years, Dan? . . . Five years since we played basketball and chased girls and made noise in study hall? . . . Has it really been five years since we were 17?)*

"Remember Larry Bird and Kevin McHale? I shot the jumper and made the passes, and you posted up and grabbed the boards. Man, those were the days!"

He's forgotten about me now. He's back on the old cracked asphalt court again, with its rusty backboards and tilted rims.

He catches an imaginary pass, dribbles once, fakes right and pivots left, jumps, and fades. His arm comes out to full extension, and the wrist snaps down

*(waving good-bye)*

111

just like he showed me a hundred summers ago on the playground.

*(It's still easy for you, isn't it? . . . Just like everything else . . . still natural . . . and I'll bet the girls are all cheering too. Still cheering five years later . . . )*

He skips away from the imaginary basket, and now he's the referee, hand in the air, signaling the scorekeeper to count the basket. A factory looms behind him, a dull red backdrop for his solitary game.

I lean against a dirty blue Camaro and stare up at the drab walls. Cracked, dusty windows stare back blankly. A tiny single door stands propped open—just a keyhole in a huge red-brick wall.

People begin to pour out in a steady stream, jostling and laughing, human drops of water leaking

*(escaping)*

from a red-brick bucket. Shouts float across the parking lot, scrambled and disembodied.

" . . . where you eatin'?" " . . . be back by noon" " . . . you comin', man?" " . . . thank God for lunch hour" " . . . hurry up, will ya? . . ."

*(You don't really work here, do you, Dan? . . . You could get lost in a place like this . . . And nobody ever cheers for factory workers . . . )*

"Hey, man, didja know I might be gettin' married?" His voice snaps me back to reality.

I shake my head.

"Yeah, me an' Jenny. We're gonna get our own apartment pretty soon. I just got a raise here—almost a dollar an hour—so I'm makin' over eight bucks an hour now.

*(You were going to play for the Celtics, remember? . . . A couple hundred grand a year and your own sporting goods store . . . Going to retire when you're 35 . . . )*

"The boss says I'm a good worker, so maybe I can make it to floor foreman . . ." His voice trails off. He grins apologetically and shrugs. "Hey, it ain't the Celtics, but it's better than mowin' lawns for the rest of my life, right? Mowin' lawns or pumpin' gas."

His gaze settles on my penny loafers. "College man, huh?

*112*

That always was your thing. It was easy for you, ya know, schoolwork and all that."

*(That's what you always thought, wasn't it? . . . Just because I got good grades, it must have been easy for me, right? . . . Hate to disappoint you . . . )*

"I coulda never made it in college. I never got into studyin' like you did. I mean, it was like you *loved* to read that junk, ya know, Shakespeare an' everything."

I can hear the same note of scorn I used to hear in high school.

*(You still don't get it, do you, Dan? . . . That's where I could be the best . . . You had the basketball court and the baseball diamond and the football field and a dozen girls following you everywhere . . . I had the classroom . . . It wasn't a fair exchange—not fair at all . . . )*

He grins again. "I tried a few times, ya know? Remember when I was failin' that history class and I came to you for help? An' you got all steamed and kept tellin' me 'Look, Dan, ya gotta study the stuff?' Right, like I was gonna start studyin' all of a sudden. I needed more help than that!" He laughs.

*(Is that what you wanted? Just some help? . . . Or did you want me to give you some magic formula so it would be easy for you, like everything else? . . . Maybe then everybody could have cheered for you in the classroom, too . . . )*

He shrugs, dismissing the subject, and grins. "Hey, man, remember when we won the basketball tournament? You still got your trophy?"

I nod.

*(Yeah, I've still got it . . . Two months of practice . . . hour after hour of passing and shooting . . . all for an eight-inch plastic trophy . . . I don't know why, but I've still got it . . . )*

His eyes light up. "Yeah, I've still got mine, too." He shakes his head. "Man, those were the days."

He stretches, and looks up at the sky. A little cottonball cloud slides across the sun, obscuring it for a moment, and he looks back at me. His eyes have a faraway look.

"You couldn't figure it out, could ya? I mean, why I wanted to win that tournament so bad. You couldn't figure out why I kept draggin' ya out there to practice."

*(No. I didn't understand it . . . I still don't . . . Everybody knew you were the best . . . You didn't need that tournament to*

*prove it . . . And there were a dozen other guys who would have jumped at the chance to be on your team . . . I only played for fun . . . You'd been playing all your life . . . )*

"But we were a team, ya know? The Boys. It sounds like kindergarten, but we were best friends. We *had* to play together."

Embarrassed, he stops, jams his hands in his pockets, and stares at the ground. He continues slowly.

"Basketball was my thing, you know, something I was really good at. It was the only thing I could teach you—like how it felt to spin off a pick and drop a 15-foot jumper. That's the only thing I had . . ."

*(The only thing you had? . . . Dan, I thought you had everything!)*

A huge void of silence opens up between us, and the voices of the returning factory workers rush in to fill it.

Dan comes out of his reverie suddenly, grins, and claps his hands. He's back on the imaginary court again, and this time he brings me along with him. He looks away and whips the ball to me behind his back—and even though it's been five years

*(forever)*

since we practiced this play, my body remembers what to do.

I spin left, give my invisible defender a head fake, come back around right, and bang it in off the backboard. And Dan is the referee again, already there to signal the basket and whistle the foul. We're both grinning this time . . .

*(Yeah, we're a team all right, no two ways about it . . . )*

But then another whistle blows. It's only the mournful sound of a small town noon whistle, but it steals his smile, slumps his shoulders, and makes him five years older . . .

*(We're both 21 now, almost 22 . . . Adults . . . Will I ever get used to that?)*

Suddenly the little cottonball cloud comes back with all its friends and hides the sun.

He looks toward the factory, then turns to me. "Gotta get back, man. Sure has been good seein' ya again."

He stands still for a moment, head cocked to one side. "You just about got it made, I guess. Not that that's any surprise. I wish somebody woulda convinced me to go to college. Wouldn't that've been somethin'? Dan the college man."

He laughs hollowly. "Well, I gotta go. Wish I could hang out for a while, but duty calls. Sorry, man."

He heads toward the factory. And I want to call him back and tell him that I'm sorry too
*(sorry for so many things)*
but it's too late now. He's too far
*(five years)*
away, and the factory swallows him.

♦ ♦ ♦

# Cotton

## *Diana Sauerwein*

I STARTED from sound sleep, heart pounding and mouth dry. Who'd called me?

I strained to see in the darkness, to hear some sound. I was sure someone had shouted my name. The soft mound that was my husband moved ever so slightly with the rhythmic breathing of sleep. He was obviously undisturbed by whatever had awakened me. Quieted by his gentle slumbering, I lay back on the pillows, but I still felt a sense of urgency.

I wondered why I, an unusually sound sleeper, had been awakened in the middle of the night for no apparent reason.

Suddenly the name Cotton rang in my ears as insistently as if it had been audible.

*God, where is he? What's the matter?*

I hadn't seen Cotton for 20 years.

We'd been best friends, Cotton and I, drawn together like the outcasts of Poker Flat. Our respective family circumstances were generally regarded as disgraceful by the largely German community where we lived, and cruel words often punctuated our experiences at the local church school. So our friendship became the shield that protected us from sarcasm and rejection.

We traded school pictures and chose each other for our baseball teams. We played hide-and-seek, fearless in the darkness of the summer nights. Barefooted, we walked the polished rails, waiting for the train, sometimes pressing our ears to the warm steel, listening importantly for the first distant rumble of the westbound Santa Fe.

Abandoned chicken houses became hideouts for our secret club. We hid treasures there—jars of sawdust (it smelled so woodsy), glistening rocks, smooth peeled sticks, matches, and scribbled notes folded to resemble some crude form of origami. We rode our bikes over every road in town, explored every alley. We dug caves in dirt banks and camouflaged them with leaves. We pretended to be frightened by make-believe ghosts in the Reubens' condemned house, empty now except for old newspapers and chicken feathers.

But mostly we just talked, sitting on the porch steps outside Cotton's house. Cotton's mother was a vast expanse of a woman named Tillie; elbow-deep in washing and ironing most of the time, she ran her household from the kitchen. Older brothers and sisters were everywhere, along with commotion, friendly clutter, and the perpetual smell of soup.

On his porch Cotton and I discussed the latest happenings in the fishbowl that was our town, recounting with wide-eyed curiosity the events that captured our imagination. Tales of tornadoes, rattlesnakes, runaway bulls, and overturned tractors—even the auto accident that decapitated Hazel, the local hairdresser. All had their place in our animated conversations. It was so easy to talk, sitting there in the sun, doodling in the dirt with our peeled sticks. So easy to talk and dream . . .

Cotton would tilt his head back, tossing the palest blond hair out of his blue eyes. "W-e-l-l," he'd say in a slow, dreamy way, "when I grow up I'm going to have a motorcycle and I'll give you a ride. And I'm going to be a preacher, and we'll get married." At the age of 10 we had no idea of romance; getting married just seemed like a good way to stay friends forever.

Time went by, and we stayed friends, fiercely loyal. I despised the teacher who whipped Cotton with a switch from a locust tree. Cotton sat stoically in class that afternoon, bruised and covered with welts, all because he'd run into the foyer of the girls' restroom in the heat of an after-lunch game of tag. Tillie put Cotton in public school after that.

Attending different schools made it difficult to see each other, but we'd talk whenever we could. Somehow I felt we would be kids forever and friends forever. Then one day in our early teens Cotton made a silly suggestive remark, embarrassing both of us. Not knowing how to make amends and too proud to apologize, he made himself scarce, and the easy camaraderie of our younger years slipped away.

Sometimes that special friend feeling would surface. Cotton's boy-am-I-glad-to-see-you smile brightened my reluctant arrival at a Christian high school. It was good for both of us to see an old friend in a new place. Then one Saturday night an accidental collision in the gym hopelessly tangled his roller skates in my cancan petticoats, the momentum pulling yards of net across the floor. For a brief moment we were the kids of yesteryear, embarrassment drowned in peals of laughter.

In the neutral environment of school we made other friends. We dated, but never each other. We still talked when we had a chance, but that wasn't often.

Then I heard rumors that Cotton had gotten himself in trouble and was being dismissed from school. I saw him in the gym during free time, and he explained that he'd been caught off campus with his girlfriend. The next thing I knew, he wasn't there anymore. That talk in the gym was our last. Now 20 years had passed . . .

*Where is Cotton now?* I wondered, still propped against my pillows. But the dark night held no answers. I missed my friend, was concerned about the turn his life had taken so long ago, and wondered what had become of him.

"O Lord, You know where he is," I said finally. "He's not lost to You. Take care of him, keep him safe, but most of all, lead him into a lasting friendship with You." The urgency I felt was calmed by the assurance that God would answer, that it was He who'd awakened me for the very purpose of praying. I knew He loved Cotton more than I or anyone else could.

In the following months I tried to locate Cotton, but my efforts were fruitless. I'd long since moved from our hometown, and the few people with whom I still had contact seemed to know nothing about him. The only news I gathered was that he'd been a sailor in the Vietnam War, and had barely escaped with his life when his ship was destroyed in the Gulf of Tonkin. His mother had died, and the rest of his family had scattered to places unknown.

Months, years, went by. My frequent nighttime awakenings continued. In those dark hours as I prayed, my feelings of helplessness were comforted with the assurance that God would work His miracle, and that all He needed to work with even greater power was a request from someone who loved Cotton. I longed to tell Cotton that I hadn't forgotten him, that I wanted to see him in heaven, to see him running joyfully across the grass with that same grin I'd known when we were childhood friends.

So I continued to pray for him, and then one February I got a phone call from Uncle Bill. After bringing me up to date on the few relatives left in the old hometown, he began to ramble about himself and my aunt. "Aunt Cleoma is bringing folks over for dinner this weekend," he said. "There's going to be a baptism."

"Oh, anyone I know?" I asked casually.

"Do you remember Cotton?"

♦ ♦ ♦

# DISCOVERY

*What is it that makes life so surprising? We sometimes think we have it just about figured out and then—wham. A new twist. Another viewpoint. A stunning reversal.*

*The discoveries in these stories touch our emotions, from deep grief to sparkling ecstasy. "You'll Be Happy There" may be the most powerful story from our first 20 years, in terms of the response it generated. And "The Window" is a multi-reprinted classic. In fact, all the stories in this section merit a sign at the entrance:*

**HANG ON. ADVENTURE AHEAD.**

♦ ♦ ♦

# The Woman at the Well

## *Gary B. Swanson*

THE door swung open, clattering against the wall, and the woman hurried in.

A man rolled over on the bed, scowling in the sudden sunlight. "Where is your jar?" he asked. "I thought you'd gone for water."

The woman's face glowed with the heat of the waning afternoon—or was it something else? He couldn't tell.

"I have no further need for water," she said breathlessly.

He rolled his eyes. "You and your riddles!"

She laughed. "I've seen the Messiah."

The man looked at her more closely. "Have you indeed? You went out for water and you found the Messiah."

"He is at Jacob's well."

"Just sitting there passing the afternoon, is He?"

The woman turned abruptly serious. "Don't mock me! I know what I've seen."

"Why are you so sure that He is the Messiah?"

"He knows my whole life. He knows of my marriages. He knows of you and me . . ."

"Everyone in Sychar knows of you and me; there's nothing remarkable in that."

"But no one else has known the desperation we've admitted only to each other—the times we've clung together, weeping in the darkness."

The man turned away. "You swore you would tell no one of that."

She sat down next to him—reached out and touched his shoulder. "I didn't tell Him; He told me. It seems He knows us better than we do ourselves. He knows what we want—what we *really* want."

"What do we really want?"

"You will know that when you see Him."

"I am not a religious man . . ."

She took his hand and led him toward the door. "That is just the part that is most thrilling—neither is He."

♦ ♦ ♦

# You'll Be Happy There

## *Maria Anne Hirschmann*

THE nearly naked trees reached in shadows through the bedroom window. He couldn't sleep. Well, who could, knowing that tomorrow your whole life would be changed. Academy—that was a funny name for a school. Sounded like soldiers' uniforms and marching drills. Tomorrow he was going to academy.

He watched shadows on the wall and thought about academy, and wished he could sleep. He sat up. His long bony legs hung over the edge of the bed and rested in two big, bare feet on the floor.

What would a Christian school be like? What kind of place was it where people didn't make fun of you? Where you could be yourself and not be ashamed or afraid?

Maybe a sandwich and glass of milk would help him get to sleep. He headed for the refrigerator.

"Carl, what are you doing up?" His grandma's voice startled him. She was sitting at the table.

"What are *you* doing up?"

She laughed. "Guess we're both pretty excited." She hadn't turned on the light, and the moonlight fell through the window above the sink, making abstract symbols on the linoleum floor. "It will be so wonderful, Carl," the old woman was saying. He added some lettuce to the sandwich, and a slice of tomato, and some cheese.

"Yes, but—" he started to speak, but was afraid to say it.

"But what?" she asked. "You still want to go, don't you?"

"Yes, but I was just wondering—" He hesitated. "What if the kids don't like me?"

No one ever had. He was almost used to it. It was just one of those facts of life. No one had ever liked him, except Grandma of course. She was different.

"They'll like you, Carl," she said confidently. "It's a good school, I told you. They teach Bible there. The kids will be different. You'll see."

Her voice rambled on.

No one had ever liked him. And he knew it was his fault. He didn't mean to be the way he was—different, and all that. But he couldn't help it.

He was clumsy and slow and afraid of people. That's why he didn't talk much. He just grinned. When he was scared or nervous or embarrassed or hurt, he grinned.

His father had hated that grin. Hated it so much that he broke Carl's nose because of it. That was when Carl was little, before his dad disappeared. Carl hated the grin too, but he couldn't stop his lips from curling whenever he felt uncomfortable, which was often.

He'd even grinned at his mother's funeral, with the neighbors whispering "suicide" all around him. He had been scared and lonely and had wanted to die too—but he grinned.

"No heart," the women had said. "No feelings at all. He is one big reason for her death. Poor woman, she never wanted that child in the first place."

The words didn't bother him much anymore. They used to, but not now. He'd gotten used to remarks like that. It was just part of his life.

He took a long drink of milk. The cold liquid felt good on his hot throat.

"Another thing, Carl." Grandma was still talking. She stood up, and put a soft arm around him. "I wouldn't let you go somewhere if I didn't think you'd be happy there." She shuffled out of the kitchen, her hands guiding her more than her eyes.

She had never cared how clumsy he was, or how much he grinned. If she thought the kids would like him, they probably would. And suddenly he wanted to go so much that he ached. He wanted to be with kids who liked him. He wanted to be happy.

The principal smiled. "Well, Carl, we can certainly give you a try. We need someone at our school farm. You may work up to 30 hours a week if you wish."

Carl's heart somersaulted.

"If you maintain good grades, we may be able to get a scholarship or some other financial help for you."

Carl stood in front of the desk, his long, dangling arms ending in nervous fists, his large ears protruding from under a fresh home haircut. He tried to thank the principal, but all he could do was nod and grin.

And Carl moved into the dorm.

The excitement of being in a new world hit him all at once, in his stomach. It felt like feathers. He'd never been at a Christian school before, never been where people liked him. He wanted to soak it all in—all the happiness and goodness, and Christianness of the place.

The farm was big, and Carl knew he'd enjoy working there. He liked doing things with his hands. Liked the smell of earth and cows and hay.

And there was a pond. It looked almost like a picture, with the sunlight skipping around on it, and the bushes and trees clustering near its edge. He stood listening to the water and watching it change with every gust of wind.

The day began at 4:00 a.m. with milking. Then worship and breakfast. Carl didn't mind worship. He didn't always understand it, but he didn't mind it.

He usually sat in the same place, the end seat in the third row. It was rather odd, but nobody else ever sat in that row. He didn't know why. Maybe it was tradition.

One morning he decided to sit in the fourth row. That morning, nobody sat in the fourth row.

He hadn't really expected the students to come running to him with open arms. But at least nobody was making fun of his grin or beating him up.

Some of the kids laughed at him because he was so old—17 and in the ninth grade. He ignored them. But sometimes he did feel lonely.

He saw his roommate talking with the dean one day, holding his nose and saying something about the smell of a barnyard. Later the dean asked Carl if he'd like to have a small room all to himself, at reduced rent, of course.

"It's not too big, and you can't lock the door," the dean said, looking at the floor. "But you will be able to set your own schedule. And, well, it would be more private."

Carl accepted. "Thank you for your kindness," he said. He felt good, knowing now he wouldn't bother anyone when he got up so early in the morning.

John, a senior who lived across the hall from Carl's new room, helped him move. No one had ever helped Carl do anything before, and Carl was so happy and so nervous about it he didn't know what to do.

When they were finished, Carl grabbed John's hand and shook it vigorously, thanking him for helping with the move. "Glad to do it," John answered, self-consciously. Just then a boy named Rick started laughing very loudly. John turned red, and went into his room. Carl didn't see John very often after that.

The days went by. Carl's small room became the center of attention. He was so tired from working on the farm that he didn't wake up when someone entered his room. Rick and his friends sneaked in and wound wire around Carl's toes and attached the wires to an electrical outlet. The shock scared Carl half to death, but he didn't know how to react, so he just grinned.

No one talked to him between classes. No one sat in the same row with him at worship.

From day to day his grin got a bit wider and sadder. He should have known it would be that way. Should have known that people are the same everywhere.

Fall Week of Prayer came. At the end of the week there was

a call. Rick and some of his friends went forward. Lots of girls went forward. Carl grinned.

John started forward. He contemplated inviting Carl to go with him. But he remembered Rick's loud laughter. And he thought of the snickering girls who held their noses whenever they referred to Carl. He hesitated near Carl's chair as he headed up the aisle. Hesitated, but didn't stop. Carl stayed in his chair.

Following the Week of Prayer, things changed. Rick had been "converted," and he was now very friendly with Carl.

Having a friend was a brand-new experience for him. Rick talked to him between classes. Sometimes he walked from the dining room to the dorm with him. Sometimes he even came to Carl's room to talk.

And Carl's loneliness disappeared. He thought about Rick a lot. He thought about him when he was working on the farm and while he was studying. He even prayed for Rick one night. And Carl hardly ever prayed. It's just that he'd never had a real friend before, and he wanted to thank God for Rick.

It wasn't long before Rick told him about Berta. Berta was big and fat and a bit sloppy. She had no dates or friends. Carl felt sorry for her. Then Rick told him a secret. Berta liked Carl.

Carl was stunned. How could a girl like him? But Rick knew, and as a friend, he told Carl.

And on the other side of campus, Rick's girlfriend, Jennifer, told Berta that Carl liked her. And Berta blushed.

It was fun—the joke. Most of the students were in on it. They carried fabricated messages and notes, those new friends of Carl and Berta.

Rick finally arranged a date. Open house was coming, and Rick explained all about it. He told Carl about asking Berta, showing her through the dorm, helping her to refreshments. Carl didn't know if he'd be able to do it. But after coaching from Rick, he thought he might enjoy it. He'd never had a date before.

On the day of open house he ironed his one white shirt. Then he knocked on John's door and asked to borrow his shoe polish. John gave it to him, and watched Carl leave with a new spring in his step.

John didn't like Rick's idea, but he had to admit it was quite a joke.

When Carl brought the polish back on his way to the shower

and humbly thanked him for his great kindness, John looked a bit uneasy. "Don't mention it, man," he said. Carl looked so happy and full of anticipation that John decided to be a genuine friend to him. *As soon as the open house thing is over,* he vowed to himself, *I'll start hanging around with Carl, helping him with classwork and stuff.*

Open house began. The girls wore new dresses, and flowers, and smiles. The boys all smelled like lime aftershave. There was a special glint in the eyes of some students. They watched for The Couple. But The Couple never arrived.

After some searching, Jennifer found Berta. She was in the bathroom—crying. No one had seen Carl since he returned John's shoe polish.

John and the dean headed for Carl's tiny room. His white shirt lay on the bed, smeared with black shoe polish. His clean, shining shoes sat nearby—nailed to the floor. The buttons on his sport coat had been cut off. Soon kids crowded the room to see how Rick had pulled off the biggest joke of the school year. But for some reason, nobody laughed.

A scrap of paper with Carl's scribbled handwriting lay on the desk.

"I'm so sorry that I couldn't have been a better Christian here. I wanted so much to come to this place. I know I'm hard to make friends with, but I liked every one of you. I won't forget your many kindnesses to me. Forgive me of my mistakes and good-bye."

Nobody slept that night. The faculty men searched for Carl everywhere. Early the next morning, just as the sun was turning the pond into a sea of gold, they found him. They dredged his body from the weedy bottom.

"It's a good school, I told you. They teach Bible there. The kids will be different. You'll be happy there, Carl."

◆ ◆ ◆

# From One About to Be Murdered

## *Karl Haffner*

**N**OVEMBER 29
Dear diary,

I was adopted today! Don't write me in care of the orphanage. Send all letters to the Red Lodge Ranch in Scobey, Montana, where the deer and the buffalo—and I—roam! The O'Brians examined every orphan before they *finally* chose "yours truly." I supposed it was my youth and vigor that sold them. Guess what? I finally have a real live brother—Travis. My mind explodes with excitement. God has truly blessed me.

**December 1**
Dear diary,

God has truly cursed me. I discovered the reason I was adopted into the O'Brian family—to be murdered. I overheard Mr. O'Brian talking with Travis today when they were stacking hay.

"It's up to you, son, to see to it that we have us a mighty fine Thanksgiving meal this next year."

"I know, Dad."

"Takes a lot of dedication to rightly tend a turkey all year, ya know."

"Yes sir."

"You got to feed him."

"I will."

"And play with him."

"Depend on me, Pop."

"And protect him every day. That way when you butcher Stanley he'll make the finest Thanksgiving meal in these here parts."

*Stanley*. I hate my name.

126

**December 3**

Dear diary,

I'm starting to make this my home. My daily chore is helping Trav take one penny out of a bowl. He says it's his "countdown" till he graduates from eighth grade. I suppose I could do the same thing for my life, but I'm not looking forward to an empty bowl like Trav is.

**December 5**

Dear diary,

I try not to think about it. Trav sure does take good care of me. Today we trekked across a fresh blanket of silky snow. I'm gonna be happy here—for 356 days anyway.

**December 25**

Dear diary,

Christmas. Hot apple cider, popcorn balls, Ritz crackers with cheddar cheese—do these Homo sapiens know how to party or what?

You should've smelled the gingerbread cookies in the oven. And heard the squeal of delight when Trav opened his new Pioneer stereo system. Or felt the warmth of the pine crackling in the fireplace.

They even remembered me in their festivities. Mr. and Mrs. O'Brian gave me a whole box of Honey Nut Cheerios! Trav gave me a turquoise bow tie. He fastened it to my wattled neck, and I pranced around the Christmas tree, squawking with delight. I've never seen Mrs. O'Brian laugh so hard in all my life! Her tears of laughter mixed with her mascara, and her eyes looked like a coon's.

The last thing I remember was drifting to sleep, cuddled in Trav's lap, while he was watching *The Hunchback of Notre Dame*.

**January 15**

Dear diary,

Trav and I tiptoed across the frozen creek today. He told me how much he likes Thora. He showed me a picture. She's a cute redhead just like Trav. He's not sure if he can take all the teasing about her freckles. I didn't know what advice to give, so I just

127

listened. I hope he gets this worked out within 315 days. Because after that I won't be here to listen.

**February 7**
Dear diary,

Mr. and Mrs. O'Brian left for a mini-vacation to Texas. Trav and I have Red Lodge Ranch all to ourselves! Trav played hooky from school today so we could ice-skate on Cricket Pond.

**February 10**
Dear diary,

With the folks out of town, Trav said, "C'mon, Stanley, now we can roast marshmallows in the wood stove!"

We were thoroughly absorbed when a marshmallow ignited. In a flash a paper plate burst into flames. The blazing plate flopped into the trash can, which exploded into a geyser of smoke.

"You all right, Stanley?" Trav asked me. "Oh, looks like you just toasted your front feathers a bit."

Trav found some ointment that soothed the pain. I sure love that guy for taking such good care of me.

I get so depressed when I think of the short time. Never mind.

**March 28**
Dear diary,

Trav took me to town with him today. He got me a Baby Ruth candy bar from Martha's 5 & 10 store. I felt guilty eating a baby. Poor Ruth's family.

**May 16**
Dear diary,

I won first place! I couldn't believe it!

I wasn't too excited about entering the Finest Fowl contest at the annual county jamboree. But Trav insisted. So I just stood proud—proud to have the finest owner in the county. Wouldn't you know it? Before I could blink, I had three blue ribbons plastered to my feathers! Trav hugged me so hard I like to have choked to death. He screamed, "We did it, Stanley, we did it!"

Thora ambled in our direction to see what the commotion was about. Her gaze met Trav's. I held my breath. This was the first time I'd actually seen Thora—though I knew all about her.

"I see you won all three categories." She grinned, and I saw her avocado-green eyes Trav talks about.

"Well . . ." Travis was turning red like the wattle under my chin. "It wasn't me; it was Stanley."

"May I pet him?"

"Sure."

I stuck my head up high, hoping to help Trav in whatever way possible.

"S'pose you got lots to do, huh?"

I could feel Trav's heart pounding like a hailstorm against my head. "No, not really. Can I, ah, would you like to, um, I was thinkin' if you weren't helping your mom at the pie booth, you could come with, ah, Stanley and me to get some cotton candy. Stanley loves cotton candy."

I had never tasted cotton candy.

"I'd be much obligated." I think she was trying to sound like a grown-up, and meant to say *obliged.*

**June 2**
Dear diary,

Trav graduated today! I watched from the car window—proud as a peacock. He fared as the most handsome fella in the world, marching tall in his dazzling black bathrobe! We celebrated by skinny-dippin' in Cricket Pond.

**August 5**
Dear diary,

Pastor Goodrum from church visited us. I don't know why he visited these here parts. I s'pose he came to read from the Good Book about Jesus. He told us the more we know Jesus, the less we'll ever want to hurt Him by our actions.

**August 7**
Dear diary,

Try as I might, I can't get Pastor Goodrum and that worship out of my mind. I can see how the more I get to know Travis, the less I'd ever want to hurt him. And you know what else? I really think Trav thinks the same of me. Just a gut feeling I have.

**October 18**
Dear diary,

Trav and I climbed an oak tree today. We laughed hysterically when the seat of his pants ripped out. When we got home Mrs. O'Brian had some lemonade for us. We slept in our pup tent for the last time.

**November 23**
Dear diary,

Three more days. Travis seems so depressed lately. I hope it's nothing I did. I want all the memories of his "best friend Stanley" to be happy ones.

**November 24**
Dear diary,

I overheard Mr. O'Brian and Trav talking by the telephone today. "Son, you gonna kill Stanley tomorrow or Thursday?"

I watched.

Trav's gaze dropped to his feet. "Dad, you remember what the pastor said? As we get to know someone, we accept him and love him more and more. Well, when we first got Stanley, I would have snapped the life out of him in a second. But now that I know Stanley, I don't think I can do that."

"Pastor Goodrum was talking about people, not turkeys."

"It don't make no matter, Dad. I can't kill my best friend. Besides, you don't even know Stanley."

"Travis, you know folk come from miles around every Thanksgiving to eat the best grub in the county here. I don't aim to let you ruin that reputation on account of your silly imaginings."

"Pop, please don't make me kill Stanley."

"You don't have to. If you rather me do it—"

"If you love me you wouldn't want to hurt me like that, Dad. That's what the pastor was talking about—stuff like that."

"If you prefer me to kill Stanley, I can do it tomorrow afternoon."

**November 25**
Dear diary,

Tomorrow is Thanksgiving.

November 27
Dear diary,
    Yesterday was Thanksgiving!

♦ ♦ ♦

# The French Lesson
## *Dave Sydnor*

NEW Canaan, Connecticut, 1963:
    Students called him Fishface. And I suppose that when he pronounced certain French words, there was a resemblance. But that was a by-product of the language, not the shape of his face. There really wasn't anything wrong with Mr. Powell, but in my high school that didn't matter. He was not a popular teacher. That's where I came in. I didn't need much of an excuse to dislike a teacher. Troubled by a tense and unhappy home life, I was taking it out on the entire adult world.

Compared to the tougher kids, I was merely a petty nuisance. I wasn't hard to handle. Fishface did it by isolating me: a front-row corner seat, surrounded by studious girls. I responded by folding my arms over a closed French book and staring at the chalkboard.

The "cold war" lasted for several weeks, till one day I was unexpectedly confronted. The lesson had been droning on as usual when suddenly Mr. Powell turned sharply toward me and blurted, "Don't you ever *entertain* the idea of going to France someday?"

There was a tone of exasperation in his voice. My response was immediate. Mimicking his voice, gestures, and facial expression, I turned and said, "Mr. Powell, I don't even *entertain* the idea."

The class laughed. I hoped they would. Mr. Powell himself thought it amusing. I wanted him to. The real bitterness was known only to me, and even I didn't understand it.

## Paris, France, 1944:

Armies aren't often sensitive to the romantic interests of their personnel. When armies move, soldiers move with them. In the fall of 1944, armies in Europe were on the move. In Paris, American GIs were heroes, and French girls were more appealing than the wrong end of German rifles. Romances flourished. But the armies kept moving. And romances died along the way; shot down in Belgium and Luxembourg, and along the banks of the Rhine. For the armies, there were replacements. For others it wasn't quite that easy.

## Niles, Michigan, 1977:

I was midway through my courses in seminary. The bills were staggering. Nevertheless, my wife and I wanted to celebrate our first anniversary in style. We decided to splurge at the salad bar at the nearby Holiday Inn.

In the lobby as we were leaving, a middle-aged woman touched my arm. A slightly quizzical look in her eye made me think she might be lost. In a way, she was.

She was alone, on her first visit to the United States. No one had met her at the airport. She spoke no English, only French. Communication was awkward. I'd been to France twice since high school, but my French was still atrocious. Sensing that I wanted to help, she pointed to the pay phone, then held out a worn piece of paper with a rough hand-drawn map.

"Taxeee," she said politely, then something I didn't understand.

I helped myself to a closer look at the map as she watched me with interest. The map was sketchy, but it was indeed Niles, Michigan. Whatever she was looking for wasn't far away.

"Taxeee?" she said again.

I liked this woman, somewhat stocky and plain-featured, neat, simply dressed. She was no tourist. I looked at the map again.

"No," I said, "No taxeee. *Nous trouvons*" ("We find").

Her smile of relief, appreciation, and excitement increased my determination. Actually there was no problem. The map was simple but more than adequate. It pointed to a small, quiet cemetery outside of town.

By the time we arrived, we'd learned several things, in spite of my pitiful French. We knew her name—Genevieve. And where she was from—Paris. And how in 1944 she met an American GI and fell in love.

They were engaged, but never married. The army moved on. They would have to wait. But then a bullet, or an artillery shell, or something broke off the engagement. She'd never married. For more than 30 years she'd been saving up to visit the grave of the man she loved. How she got that map I'll probably never know. I forgot to ask.

Trying to be polite, we waited near the entrance while Genevieve walked among the rows of graves. Along the stone wall at the back, she stopped in the shade of a large oak. I knew right away she'd found it. I tried to look away, but I couldn't. Anyway, she didn't notice.

I'd sort of expected a mushy, gushy scene, but it wasn't that way at all. She just looked down with a quiet tenderness and dignity that almost tore me apart. I wondered how they had met. It was no barroom pickup, that was certain. It was in her eyes. Those people had known each other. She wiped a single tear from her cheek. Her folded hands seemed to nudge forward just a bit, then relaxed. I started to lose it and had to look away. But songbirds and crab apple trees in full bloom and the radiance of spring only made it worse.

Suddenly I longed to tell her about God's love, and what she meant to Him, and all He had for her and wanted to give her, but I couldn't. I groped for the words, but they weren't there. They were stuck in a closed French book under folded arms, 14 years away. I could only reflect on my own past 30 years, as I knew Genevieve must be reflecting on hers. Opportunities lost. Hers through no fault of her own. But mine through bitterness, foolishness, and pride.

And now? Well, if only I'd known. But it just doesn't work that way. What else can I say? "I'm sorry, Mr. Powell. I'm sorry, Genevieve. I'm sorry, Lord."

◆ ◆ ◆

# Handful of Nails

## C. V. Garnett

SPRING seemed to have cast lots with summer and lost by a thin margin. The heat was of summer, but a young breeze played during the nights over the newly plowed fields.

In a shop at the edge of the town, a carpenter wiped his brow with a practiced hand. With him worked his son, whose thoughts and questions were the same as many of today's sons, though this was indeed many years ago.

The father answered as best he could.

"What you shall be, son, depends upon many things, the chief of which is yourself. What do you *wish* to be?"

"Not a carpenter," the boy answered, perhaps too quickly. The father placed a long beam upon the floor, then straightened himself. His long look voiced the sorrow of his silence.

"I'm sorry, Father. It is not my wish to hurt you. You do good work, and from miles around do people come to ask it of you. But I wish to do more, be more."

If there were tears in the eyes of the father, his son did not see them. The strong hand had turned back to hammer and bench and resumed pounding a handful of nails into their predestined places. After a moment, he was able to turn back to his son and the subject.

"Son," he began, "when I was 12, a long time ago, I hoped to carve not wood but destiny. But life, as you may learn, is not always as we would have it. And knowing the beams and boulders that rose to barricade my way, I make apology to no man." Then he added tenderly, "Nor boy."

"But I—"

"Not even to my son," the man hastened to add.

"I know, my father, but—"

"If I have not given you all of your desires, I have tried to provide for your needs."

"Yes, Father, and I do not mean to sound ungrateful. I am

134

grateful to you and to Mother—rest her soul—but I wish to make you proud."

"A good life would make me proud."

"But I mean more than that."

"I am not sure there is more than a good life."

"But you do not understand—I wish to stamp time with the imprint of my life, to nail myself firmly to the beam of history."

"Son, you know that I have saved much of my earnings for the day when you might attend the best rabbinical schools in the land. You can be a physician or teacher or whatever you choose. You need not be a lowly carpenter if you will not."

The father let that settle in, as he hoisted another beam to the bench. The boy was silent for a moment.

"Is it wrong, Father, to want to be important to others?"

"Not in itself," the man answered, "but what do you want people to know? That is the question. I hope you will find, as I have, that self-exultation is not the path to greatness or a full life. It is in service that we find happiness."

The boy watched his father. He saw his father's brow sprout beads of sweat as he crafted a cabinet someone else would enjoy. Then the boy busied himself, not so much to complete a task as to provide excuse for his silence. When the noise of pounding hammer cleared the air, he walked to the open window and inhaled deeply.

"I am doing this badly, my father. Many things wanted I to say, but I fear my words are coming backwards."

"Strangers must select words; we need but say them."

"Then tell me, Father, where is your reward? What is your satisfaction?"

"That of a task well done. Perhaps you think that simple and pagan, but when the race is ended and the search completed, what have we left but the satisfaction of tasks well done?"

The answer did not satisfy the boy. The man tried a new tack.

"There are opportunities every day to choose between right and wrong, to cast a die for the good, the true. Just last week a representative of the Roman government came into the shop and requested that I carve a special cross on which to crucify some troublemaker. I refused. And my words smote him in the face as I refused. Death, I told him, should rest in the hands of God, not man. It is God alone who has power to judge and to take life. To crucify a man because his thoughts are not those of him who holds the scepter is not God's justice." The father laughed. "You should have seen his face, son. He stormed out with threats to return with a legion and have me hanged on the very cross I refused to make. I laughed at him."

"You did well, my father. You showed courage." Silence filled the shop. The boy walked to the open window and searched the distant landscape. "It must be terrible, crucifixion," he said. "Have you ever seen a man crucified, Father?"

"Yes, once, and that a long time ago. Yet I can see it still as it if were yesterday." The man shivered.

"I hope," the boy said, "that I shall never have to see one."

"I hope you never will, also, my son."

And then to change the subject, the father said, "Enough of this sad speaking. Tell me, son, more of your dreams."

"I was thinking, Father, that maybe I will find my place in religion. Perhaps in the Temple." He turned to his father, his enthusiasm restored. "Maybe in this way I shall come into my own. Who knows but that the awaited Messiah will come in my time, and I shall have a part in His work. Perhaps my name shall be written and recorded in the scroll of the Scriptures."

"That would indeed be wonderful, son. My years are numbered. I shall likely be gone before you reach your certain destiny, but I know that you shall make me proud. Yes," and the old man's voice cracked, "I know that you shall make me more proud of you than I have made you of me."

When he regained his voice, the father chuckled.

"All this serious talk," he said. "Now go to the house and see if your sister has the supper ready, while I clean up this old shop of ours . . . of mine."

"Yes, Father."

"Oh," the father said, "and take this repaired chair to your sister; she wanted it to—"

But the boy was gone. He had dropped a handful of nails to the floor and disappeared through the open doorway.

The father hobbled to the door and called after his son.

"Judas! The chair! You forgot the chair, Judas! Come back!"

But the boy could not hear. He was too far away.

♦ ♦ ♦

# The Window

## G. W. Target

THERE were once two men, both seriously ill, in the same small room of a great hospital. Quite a small room, just large enough for the pair of them—two beds, two bedside lockers, a door opening on the hall, and one window looking out on the world.

One of the men, as part of his treatment, was allowed to sit up in bed for an hour in the afternoon (something to do with draining the fluid from his lungs), and *his* bed was next to the window.

But the other man had to spend all *his* time flat on his back—and both of them had to be kept quiet and still. That was the reason they were in the small room by themselves, and they were grateful for peace and privacy—none of the bustle and clatter and prying eyes of the general ward.

Of course, one of the disadvantages of their condition was that they weren't allowed to do much: no reading, no radio, certainly no television. They had to keep quiet and still, just the two of them.

So they used to talk for hours and hours—about their homes, their jobs, their hobbies, their childhood, what they had done during the war, where they'd been on vacations—all that sort of thing. Every afternoon, when the man in the bed next to the window was propped up for his hour, he would pass the time by describing what he could see outside. And the other man began to live for those hours.

The window apparently overlooked a park, with a lake, where there were ducks and swans, children throwing them bread and sailing model boats, and young lovers walking hand in hand beneath the trees. There were flowers and stretches of grass, games of softball, people taking their ease in the sunshine, and right at the back, behind the fringe of trees, a fine view of the city skyline.

The man on his back would listen to all of this, enjoying every minute . . . how a child nearly fell into the lake, how beautiful the girls were in their summer dresses, then an exciting ball game, or a boy playing with his puppy. Before long he could almost *see* what was happening outside.

Then one fine afternoon, when there was some sort of parade, the thought struck him. Why should the man next to the window have all the pleasure of seeing what was going on? Why shouldn't *he* get the chance?

He felt ashamed, and tried not to think like that, but the more he tried the worse he wanted a change. He'd do *anything!*

In a few days he had turned sour. *He* should be by the window. And he brooded, and couldn't sleep, and grew even more seriously ill—which none of the doctors understood.

One night as this man stared at the ceiling, the man next to the window suddenly woke up, coughing and choking, the fluid congesting in his lungs, his hands groping for the button that would bring the night nurse running. But the other man watched without moving.

The coughing racked the darkness . . . on and on . . . choked off . . . then stopped . . . the sound of breathing stopped . . . and the other man continued to stare at the ceiling.

In the morning the day nurse came in with water for their baths and found the man next to the window dead. The attendants took his body away, quietly, no fuss.

As soon as it seemed decent, the remaining man asked if he could be moved to the bed next to the window. And they moved him, tucked him in, made him quite comfortable, and left him alone to be quiet and still.

The minute they'd gone, he painfully and laboriously propped himself up on one elbow and looked out the window.

It faced a blank wall.

◆ ◆ ◆

# Madness in the Marketplace

*Stuart Tyner*

**A**ND don't run with the eggs in your basket!"

Joanna didn't hear her mother. She was close enough to hear, but familiarity with the command closed her ears. She continued running up the hill in the direction of the market.

The trip to the market was the highlight of Joanna's week. It provided hours of freedom from the boredom of her regular routine.

There was excitement at the market that filled her with a sense of adventure. All the different languages being spoken. The shouting matches between the vendors and the customers. The push and shove of women trying to grab the best cut of meat or the biggest bunch of garlic. The noisy pleas of the animals for freedom. Joanna loved it.

The farther up the hill Joanna walked, the more crowded the market became. And the bigger the crowd, the higher the asking prices.

So as usual, Joanna had managed to purchase everything she needed before she entered the most expensive stretch of market. The animals purchased here were for sacrifice in the Temple.

It was most convenient, Joanna thought. A stranger could walk all this way without having to drag along a reluctant creature, and at the very last moment buy just what he needed for the service. Even if the prices were so much higher than just down the block.

Joanna was standing at one end of this high-price section of the market when a commotion began at the other end. She looked up just in time to jump out of the way of a couple of vendors who were obviously in a great hurry. Clutching her basket and its precious contents, Joanna peered around the side of a very large Syrian woman and gazed wide-eyed at what she saw.

Dozens of vendors were now stampeding down the aisle of the market. Some of them carried folding tables and baskets filled with animals. Some dragged bundles behind them. And some had dropped everything and were just running.

Knocked-over tent poles fell in every direction. Stacks of goods toppled and crashed. Bleating animals scampered free. Coins clattered throughout the market, and people dove after them.

Suddenly the cause of the commotion appeared in front of Joanna. It was a Man. A young Man, with plain clothes. But as He strode through the market He spoke in a voice that revealed great authority. "Get out!" He commanded. "You're turning My house into a robbers' den."

Joanna held perfectly still. The young Man walked on until He came to the end of the expensive part of the market. Then He turned around and surveyed the damage. As His eyes swept over the confused scene, He noticed Joanna still standing there, hunched and peeking through half-closed eyes.

The Man walked back to Joanna, knelt down in the street to be at her eye level, and spoke to her.

"Are you OK? Are you hurt? Did someone run into you?"

"No, thank you. I'm fine. I was just a little frightened."

"I'm glad you weren't hurt." He smiled and then began to walk away.

But He stopped, turned around, and spoke again. "You want to ask Me a question, don't you?"

Joanna blushed, but summoned enough courage to ask the question that was troubling her.

"I come to this market every week for my mother," she began. "I've never seen you here before. But I heard you say to that man that this is your house. Why did you say you live in the market?"

"What's your name?" the Man asked while He seated Himself on an overturned box.

"Joanna."

"Joanna, I was quoting Scripture when I spoke of this house. These men have forgotten what God's house is for."

"What do you mean, God's house?"

"The place God has chosen to live here on earth. The place He meets with us in a very special way. This is God's house."

"This *market* is God's house?"

"Joanna, do you know where you are?"

Joanna looked around. "Yes, sir," she answered. "I'm in the most expensive part of the market."

"No, Joanna," Jesus gently corrected. "You're standing in the court of the Temple."

◆ ◆ ◆

# The Stones Cry Out

## *René Alexenko*

THE ants go marching one by one, hurrah, hurrah." The singing drowned out the roar of the bus engine. This was our first field trip of the school year. The group, largely American, was composed of the students who had come to learn German at Seminar Schloss Bogenhofen, a small Christian college in Austria. As part of Austrian history and culture class, we were off to see how the Viennese aristocracy lived.

"The ants go marching ten by ten, the little ones stop to say 'the end' . . ."

"OK, Larry, translate that song into German." Dave's sarcasm for our fellow student's study habits met with hilarious laughter. After two months of language study, we were still unable to communicate adequately. But we took every opportunity to poke fun at others' efforts.

"It doesn't translate, Dave."

My French roommate offered her one English sentence, a shaky bridge over the language gap between us. "You guys are crazy."

Larry tried to ignore our commentary. "Cool it, everybody. I'm trying to study."

"Relax, Larry. You have the rest of your life to learn irregular German verbs." Lynette's long hair whipped in the air as she snatched Larry's book and tossed it on an overhead rack.

Music exploded over the loudspeaker. Not to be outdone, we linked arms and joined in. More hilarious laughter.

"Larry, I think a game of 'Uno' would do you some good. I'll deal." With a single movement, Lynette swept the assortment of sack lunches, coats, and cameras off a seat which now served as a table.

"Why don't you join us, Deanna?" Dave offered.

Larry frowned from behind his black mustache but accepted the cards Lynette shoved at him. "You guys don't stand a chance. You'll wish you had let me study in peace."

"Who are you kidding? I'm going to blow you all away with this hand." Dave hid a card in a seat cushion, draped his long frame over the back of a seat, and peered into everyone else's hand.

But at that moment Herr Flandera blew into the microphone, the cue for silence. A World War II veteran, his patient eyes rested on the back of the bus as he waited for the din to subside. We ignored him and continued playing.

"The first stop on our trip is Malthausen, a labor camp used during World War II," he explained.

"Ha, ha, Dave. Serves you right for cheating."

"Malthausen was an auxiliary labor camp. Prisoners, including many prisoners of war, were held here to work before they were sent to Dachau, Auschwitz, or some of the larger extermination camps." Herr Flandera spoke slowly and clearly to accommodate our limited German.

"Uno!"

The bus's engine sank into low gear as Herr Flandera continued. "The people who lived in the valley had no idea this camp was here." No trace of emotion altered his voice as he recited figures for the number of inmates, the number killed, the years the camp was in operation, and the crimes the camp directors were accused of committing.

"I wish he'd be quiet. He's disrupting our game. Who cares about some morbid concentration camp?" Lynette pouted through the next round of cards.

The bus eased to a stop.

"We're here. And I was going to win this." Larry was absorbed.

Herr Flandera led the way through gates that proclaimed "Arbeit macht frei."

*A little ironic,* I thought. *The only way work would free you here is if you literally worked yourself to death.* We trudged toward the museum, a converted barracks.

CLOSED MONDAYS. The sign was posted beside the heavy door.

"Flandera lives in Austria. You'd think he'd remember every museum in the country is closed on Monday," Dave muttered under his breath as the group assembled around our teacher, who looked toward the locked doors.

"Class, the museum will not open today. However, Malthausen has memorial gardens that contain statues erected by every country that lost prisoners here. Walk around and take some pictures. I'm sorry about the museum."

The group scattered. I headed for the white obelisk directly in front of me. The inscription was in both English and German: "To the brave British soldiers, who, after suffering torture and starvation, were murdered."

The Italians listed each of their prisoners by name, complete with pictures and birth dates, on a low stone structure. Many of the prisoners had died when they were younger than I was.

I crossed the gravel path and approached the white marble structure the French had erected. There was a bit more reverence in every step. Fresh flowers adorned the altar in the semi-enclosed structure. Burned-out candles lined a narrow shelf.

I walked on, feeling more and more dwarfed by the huge bronze statues. Poles and Bulgarians had each erected deeply emotional, almost melodramatic statues. Sunken eyes stared at me out of the hollow face of a starving human. A group of prisoners with clenched fists and squared jaws raised their arms in defiance, protesting silently. I shivered in the chill of the November air.

After 20 minutes of photographing the memorials, our group left the gardens and followed a path that led through a forest. The prisoners had once marched through these dark woods each day on their way to the work quarry below. Deanna caught up with me as we entered the woods.

My eye caught the plaque of a small memorial everyone else had missed. Deanna and I translated the inscription on the simple stone altar as the group wandered away. "In eternal memory of the sons and fathers of the Jewish nation, who committed no crime except being Jewish. Genesis 4:10." I wondered what the text said.

Herr Flandera was pointing out the pond directly below the cliff as Deanna and I caught up. He said the pond had been created to break the fall of prisoners who tried to end their existence with a final jump.

We entered the depths of the quarry itself, descending on the "death steps" along the far side of the cliff. The steep, irregular stairs had acquired their name because so many prisoners had died mining and laying the rocks. I felt as if I were walking on hallowed ground.

There was nothing more to see. We headed for the waiting bus. As we left the quarry I walked past the scarred walls that still bore marks of picks and hammers. Chiseled into a smooth rock face were the letters and numbers: CCCP 28.xii.44.

This time there was communication. USSR, December 28, 1944. For the first time in my life I understood my Russian heritage. I understood perfectly the message left behind by a nameless Russian soldier who may have died on the very spot I was standing on. I understood the words my father spoke often when I was a child: "Thank God you're an American."

I was fighting tears when we boarded the bus. Deanna had found a pocket Bible, and as we took our seats and picked up the unfinished card game she read aloud Genesis 4:10, the text we had wondered about in the garden. "And the Lord said, '. . . Your brother's blood is crying to me from the ground.'"

A silence had settled over the once-boisterous bus. Quietly my friends collected their cards and put them away.

I had no words; speech was impossible. My blurred eyes didn't see the hands that took my own cards and put them back into the box.

♦ ♦ ♦

# CHRISTMAS

**God became a human being.**
**What could be more astounding?**
**But amid the "13 more shopping days until" warnings**
**and the cards and wrappings and tinsel, we sometimes**
**lose sight of love and wonder and warmth.**
**These five stories will bring them back.**

◆ ◆ ◆

# Sure as Spring
## *Lori Peckham*

THERE was a little girl who believed in Santa Claus with all her heart. She just *knew* that he was there, somewhere . . . was it at the North Pole? It really didn't matter. He knew where *she* was, and that's what she liked.

He also knew if she was bad or good. She wasn't sure she liked that, but it made her want to be awfully good all of the time. When her big sister wouldn't let her in the bathroom and she wanted to pound on the door and get her into trouble, she went outside to play instead. When her mother asked her to clean up the chocolate bar that melted into the carpet because she left it there, she wanted to pout and cry and run away from home. But then she remembered the tall Christmas tree with the twinkling lights and the colorful packages, and the kind man with the soft eyes in the shopping mall.

All year long, and not just at Christmastime, she thought of him and was eager for him to come. Sometimes she wondered why he didn't come more often to see her. But she decided that he was probably very busy at the North Pole. And after all, he had his right-hand reindeer, Rudolph, and a whole host of reindeer and elves to direct in doing nice things and wrapping presents for people.

One Christmas when she was waiting in line to talk to Santa, the big boy—he must have been 10—who was sitting on Santa's lap pulled on Santa's white beard. The kind Santa told him to stop. But the boy didn't stop. He did it again, only this time he pulled the beard all the way off.

And then a terrible thing happened. Santa slapped the boy.

The whole line of waiting children hushed. They stared at Santa Claus. Then he turned red like his suit, and he put his beard back on and motioned for the next in line to come up and sit on his knee.

But no one moved toward him. And then the children started moving back, away. Suddenly the Santa stood up and stomped off the platform, yelling, "I quit! I hate kids!"

The little girl was shocked. She couldn't even move. She stood there longer than all the rest, staring at the high-back stuffed chair Santa had been sitting in. Finally her mother came out of the Hallmark store, rolls of Santa Claus wrapping paper in her arms, and she led the little girl home.

And the little girl stopped believing in Santa Claus. She didn't write him any more letters, she stopped talking to him, she didn't even leave him cookies and milk on Christmas Eve. But she did stay awake very late, listening, and she thought—it must have been near midnight—she heard something.

The next morning bright packages were under the tree, but for the first time she noticed that the smiles on the dolls were only painted. And the stuffed animals weren't real at all. Nothing seemed real anymore. And dreaming only hurt.

Her mother and father felt the little girl's forehead and sat her in front of the TV to watch the Christmas specials, but she almost wanted the Grinch and the Abominable Snowman to win for once.

After Christmas break the little girl was very naughty in school. She forgot to feed her puppy, and she was rude to her mother. She didn't like what was happening, but she didn't feel like doing anything about it. She was just too tired. And sad.

And then, as in all good Christmas stories, something good happened. It wasn't a big, dramatic event, like the Grinch's change of heart. But it was a change, as sure as spring.

The little girl got older. And she watched people a lot. She watched how they dream even when they're adults. And she watched what they dream about.

She knew she must have something to believe in that was bigger and stronger and kinder and smarter than she was. She had to know there was someone who loved her and planned wonderful surprises for her. Someone who couldn't stay away a whole year even. Someone right there with her all the time.

And then the little girl found Someone even better than Santa Claus, because this Someone was real.

And the amazing thing is that every year she believed in Him more. He was there in her heart, growing. Sometimes she thought she could even feel her heart growing larger to hold Him. And then He would spill out, and it was even better.

He gave her gifts, too. She could see them in the color red, and the swirling of leaves, and the lights of the sky. And she knew, always, that He was planning something much bigger and better than any Christmas celebration she had ever known.

And so the little girl was very happy. She had something wide and warm to believe in, a dream that wouldn't ever have to die. And she had found Someone who loved her even more than she could love Him.

♦ ♦ ♦

# Birth of a Lamb

## *Karen Spruill*

ON Christmas morning I walked to the barn. The stars were still twinkling in the predawn, and the snow squeaked beneath my steps. The frosty air jabbed my lungs with tingly fire.

I pushed hard on one of the red double doors and slipped inside. Whispering good morning to the icy-muzzled horse in his stall, I proceeded to the back of the barn.

I pushed another door and peered into the dim back room. It was so very silent that I felt a reverence peculiar only to a farmer. As my eyes adjusted to the darkness, I could see the fat sides of docile ewes lying on the floor chewing their cuds. I watched as one lifted herself slowly and moaned.

She moved about aimlessly and settled down again. So there would be lambs for Christmas! Every year the lambing season started about the end of December.

The coldness was penetrating, so I decided that it was time to move. I tugged open a bale of hay and threw it in the horse's manger. He nickered a thanks and went to work sorting it out with his nose.

As I worked to pull down more bales for the sheep, another sound pierced the quiet. It was the tomcat coming to check out the stir in his domain. With a few agile leaps he was in front of me and meowed a feline greeting. I scratched his neck and shooed him off the bale. By the time I had finished my job the morning had grown lighter.

I could see the black-faced ewe in the corner. I turned to go, but stopped when the ewe made an effort to get up. After several attempts she stood up, only to be in as much pain as when she lay down.

It was very cold, and although I had seen many lambs born before, somehow this time it was different. Hesitantly I sat down in the doorway, telling myself that I'd soon go. The old tomcat came up to me, rubbing around my back and purring.

I petted the cat and thought while I awaited the birth. I could hear the horse shuffling his hay and the ewes grinding away at theirs. What an indifferent attitude toward new life!

My eyes swept over the big beams at the top of the barn. Up there somewhere a rat scurried. The cat stopped cleaning himself for a second to look up, then continued. I noticed the drafty, barren floor that the ewe would give birth on. It was a somber, hard world for a helpless lamb to come into.

A groan from the ewe brought my thoughts back. I rubbed my numb hands and jumped up. To fight off the numbness I ran to the hayloft and pushed some hay down for easy access later. Then I went back to check on the ewe.

Clouds of steam rose from her strained breathing. Within a minute a new form appeared. I waited for a twin lamb, but there was none. By instinct the mother made herself busy licking the lamb. It didn't take long before he was up and shivering on wobbly legs.

148

"Merry Christmas," I smiled as I slid the door shut and went outside. The sun was an orange ornament in the eastern sky behind the barn. A row of cheeping sparrows clung to the barnyard gate and signaled the beginning of another day.

A new lamb had come to the earth.

◆ ◆ ◆

# Accounts Payable

*Lee Mellinger*

AS sales manager of AIF Corporation, Jonathan Burroghson had to answer only to the vice president and the board of directors. His days were spent in meetings discussing changes in the prime rate and trying to predict the quarterly profit margin.

It was a busy life. Work started at 6:00 a.m. with the *Wall Street Journal* and a review of the day's schedule. At 8:00 a.m. there was a salesmen's meeting, followed by a board meeting. Then a meeting with the president, then a finance meeting.

When the vice president retired, Jonathan was the obvious replacement. That also made him chairman of the sales committee. More meetings, more conventions. Jonathan hardly noticed the Christmas season approaching.

But he had worked hard to get to this point. He had come from a small Midwest town and had paid his own way through college, graduating at the top of his class. He had been awarded a scholarship for graduate study at Harvard University, which gave him his pick of top management jobs.

But somewhere between Harvard and the boardroom, he had all but forgotten that life was more than AIF Corporation and maintaining a good profit margin.

But AIF had another influential member who had not forgotten life's meaningfulness. Her name was Marianne.

Everyone knew Marianne. She was the secretary in Accounts Payable, but she was welcome everywhere in the company. She offered a dose of serenity amid the industrial chaos. She was always smiling and had a peculiar habit of bringing people small gifts at crucial moments.

Giving people things made them happy, and she liked that—to see them pause and smile. Christmas was her favorite time of the year.

On the day before Christmas the board was discussing sales strategies for the coming year. "Sales bring profits, and that's what matters," Jonathan was telling his men. Suddenly the door opened. In walked Marianne.

Interrupting a board meeting was a class-one offense. No one could imagine how she got past the secretary. But there she was, smiling as if she were coming to her own birthday party.

"Hi, Mr. Burroghson. I brought your Christmas gift," she said, prancing to the front of the room and handing him a wrapped package.

Jonathan forced a smile. "Thank you, Marianne."

"I think you're going to like it," she said.

The board members were hushed.

"Aren't you going to open it?" she asked.

Jonathan glanced at the faces around the table.

"It's all right; you can open it before Christmas," Marianne urged.

Jonathan looked down at the package in his hands, then carefully pulled the red tissue paper apart. Inside were three brightly colored packages of flower seeds.

Suddenly he smiled, not his forced corporate smile but a genuine one that warmed everyone in the room. "I think this meeting can wait until after the holidays," he announced. "After all, it's Christmas Eve!"

His men hesitated, then began to gather papers into their briefcases.

Jonathan turned to Marianne. "Do you know what a profit margin is, Marianne?"

"No," she answered.

"Good, let's keep it that way." He smiled as he held the door open for her.

◆ ◆ ◆

# Redemption

## *Christopher Blake*

THEY had covered 80 miles. From Nazareth it had taken five days.

For most of the miles Mary walked; the burro jounced too heavily when she rode. Occasionally she mounted it to relieve the pressure in her swollen feet, until the jarring discomfort grew too great and she moaned to stop.

It was odd to see a woman in her ninth month of pregnancy making such a journey.

And the trip exacted its toll. Her labor began as they entered Bethlehem. Desperate, Joseph begged for a spare room—anything —for his suffering wife, but all that was left was where the animals were kept.

They took it. Joseph tied up the burro amid the mud and manure, and in one stall he spread new hay over the crusted hay. Then Mary gripped his hand fiercely and called out: no, there was no time to find a midwife. Joseph ran trembling for a flask of hot water.

Now the 80 miles of inhaling dust was over. The frantic searching was past. The agonized cries were ended.

Mary gazed at her newborn Boy. He lay in a feeding trough rimmed by boards chewed and chipped. Around Him the rank animal smells mingled with the sweet odor of old oats and barley.

Joseph brought Him to where she lay, and she unwrapped the strips of cloth that bound Him and rubbed oil on His tiny squirming body. Binding Him again, she held Him close and kissed Him, and handed Him to Joseph, who kissed Him gently and laid Him back in the trough.

Joseph sat on the hay next to Mary.

"What's wrong?" he asked.

She smiled faintly, that he should know her so well after so short a time.

"I thank God for you, and for my Son," she said.

"And . . . ?"

She bit her lower lip. "Perhaps we should have traveled faster. We might have gotten a decent room. We might have had time to fetch a midwife."

"But then you might have given birth on the way," he replied.

She sighed. "I wanted everything to be perfect."

"He's alive and healthy."

"But here? With the animals?" Her voice dripped with remorse. "Joseph, *do you know whose Son this is?*"

Joseph held her eyes. "Yes," he said finally, "I know who He is." He reached over and plucked hay from her hair. "And I know who we are also. We are doing our best."

Mary turned her face away. "Oh, Joseph," she whispered. "What can He possibly do with such a beginning?"

◆ ◆ ◆

# Because of Christmas

## *Phyllis Reynolds Naylor*

THERE were 19 people at the party—five sopranos, seven altos, four basses, and three tenors, to be exact. The annual choir get-together always drew a good turnout, but because they preferred singing to eating, there was food to spare.

Doug and Sylvia looked over the half-empty platters of egg rolls. The buffet still held trays of cookies, and a cake had gone untouched.

"What on earth are we going to do with all this food?" Sylvia said, as the door closed on the last tenor. "If the kids were coming home for Christmas this year, there would be no problem. But with just the two of us . . ."

"A block party?" Doug offered.

"Everybody's giving parties this week. Nobody needs it. I wish I could send it all to Calcutta. Such a waste."

"You don't have to go that far. *Somebody* around here ought to be able to use it."

Doug's remark set them to thinking. An orphanage, maybe. A retirement home. But how do you just drive up with a large platter of food and say, "Have some leftovers. Merry Christmas"? You don't.

"How about the night people?" Doug suggested. "Policemen, firemen, ambulance drivers . . . ? We could take it now, while it's fresh."

It was so like their young married days when—if they felt like it—they'd go sledding at midnight. Sylvia laughed.

"You're serious?"

"Why not?"

"We don't even *know* a policeman!"

"We know where to find them, don't we?"

\* \* \* \*

Jim Peterson was waiting for Car 72. It was on its way back to the station after breaking up a domestic quarrel. The officers had been roughed up a bit and would need to change clothes.

Jim felt the tension in his shoulders ease. After 16 years on the force, it should be routine by now, but it was never routine. More officers were cut up responding to marital fights than were hurt on the streets. As dispatcher, he always felt responsible.

He used to think that police work and glory were connected somehow. He used to fantasize that he'd be the neighborhood cop everyone loved, the officer who was fair, the policeman who was honest. And for 16 years he'd tried to be all those things. So what did he get?

"Pig" written on the side of his squad car, that's what. Eggs on the windshield. A brick in the middle of his back when he was trying to rescue a woman during a riot.

For some reason, the bitterness had overwhelmed him lately. What made people so vicious around Christmas, anyway? Why waste the rest of his life on a job that was unappreciated? The idea of retirement enticed him again. Get out while he was still ahead.

The station door opened, and he saw a couple coming toward him with a box. *Bomb*. That was his first idiotic thought. No, not so idiotic. They came in all kinds of containers these days.

"Merry Christmas," the woman said, smiling, setting the box down on his desk. "We just thought we'd stop by and say Thank you for being here—in case we ever need you."

Inside was a homemade cake.

\* \* \* \*

Lucy Stevens glanced at the clock as she walked through the lobby with her mop. Twelve-thirty. She wasn't supposed to go through the lobby, but at this hour no one would notice.

She rang the bell for the elevator and leaned heavily against the wall, watching the light on the panel descending. If she didn't bake cookies tonight after she got home, she might as well forget it. Maybe it was time the kids learned she couldn't be a full-time parent and a full-time employee of the Drake Hotel and still do all the things they expected of her at Christmas—especially since Charlie was gone. When you're 30, you don't think about being a widow till it happens. Charlie didn't think of it either. That's why there was no insurance. And fewer presents under the tree. That's why there would probably be no special cookies this year, either. She was bone tired.

Someone tapped her arm.

"Excuse me," said a man, "but we just wanted to wish you a merry Christmas." And he placed a plate of cellophane-wrapped cookies and sandwiches in her hands.

Lucy stared at him. There was a woman smiling at her over by the door. How did they know? Why did they care?

"M-Merry Christmas," she said, still staring, and the couple disappeared through the revolving door.

\* \* \* \*

Tom Verona wheeled the empty bus into the terminal, gave it a final pump of gas to make sure it would start again for the next shift, and leaned back against the driver's seat, letting out a weary "*Ugh.*" It was as much for what lay ahead as what was behind him. Christmas, and no place to go. Not since he'd left home saying he'd never come back. That's what was wrong with ultimatums. They were made in the heat of anger.

Still, his old man made him mad. "Back in Italy . . . ," he'd say, not once, but four or five times a day. Back in Italy Dad didn't have half the advantages he had here, but he never talked about that. All he knew was that his son was never around when he needed him. Dad didn't seem to realize there wouldn't be a color TV or a vacation at the beach or a station wagon in the driveway if Tom weren't working the night shift and as many charter trips as he could manage. This was America, the land of opportunity, but you definitely had to work for what you wanted.

What his parents wanted, though, was his time. They wanted closeness and laughter and big family dinners like back in the old country.

He sighed again. So what had he done? In the middle of an argument, he'd simply packed up and walked out. Merry Christmas. Most of what they missed in America, he discovered, he missed also. Strange what a night's sleep in a cheap hotel will do for one's perspective. Still, he had pride. He'd said he wouldn't go back. To turn around and do it now would be giving in.

He unhooked his cash box, picked up his coat from the rack above, and opened the door. As he stepped off the bus he thought he saw his parents coming across the terminal. No, this couple was younger. He was hallucinating. But what did they want at this hour? Directions, probably.

And suddenly the woman was putting something in his hands—an aluminum pie plate filled with egg rolls and other delicacies.

"Merry Christmas," she was saying. "We had a party, and more food than we could possibly eat. We'd like to share it with somebody."

And then they were gone, and he stared down at the plate in his hands, still warm from the oven. Two people he didn't even know had gone out of their way to share something with him. It was the time for sharing. Time for giving up grudges, for making peace. He walked over to the pay phone on the corner and called home.

* * * *

"Well, we did it," Sylvia said, as they drove up the dark street. "I'm sure they all thought we were crazy, but it was fun."

"Probably didn't mean a thing to any of them," Doug agreed. "But who cares? It's Christmas."

♦ ♦ ♦

# FAITH

"Now faith is the substance of things hoped for, the evidence of things not seen" (Hebrews 11:1).

That might seem less like a definition than a riddle, but this section deals in numerous riddles.

Where is the line between faith and works? How is heaven like snow? Why are the wages of sin death? What's wrong with leaving home? Who could rightfully say, "You can't kill me!"?

All are questions of faith, and all find their answers in these faith-building stories. Stories of discernment, of honesty, of courage.

And then one final question remains.

"When the Son of Man comes, will he find faith on the earth?" (Luke 18:8, NIV).

◆ ◆ ◆

# The Taste of New Wine

## Kenneth Field

THE muted sounds of dancing and laughter drifted faintly to Areli, seated in the shadows of the courtyard wall. A nearly empty wine cup sat on the table near his elbow. Only the servants hurrying back and forth with food and drink for the wedding came anywhere close to him, and they didn't pay much attention to the solitary man with the faraway look in his eyes.

Areli reached for the wine cup and cradled it in his hands. Then he shifted position so that he could look out across the countryside, away from Cana. Farmlands green with the new spring growth stretched out in the distance. He drained the cup in one swallow and hoped his hired man had remembered to do all the chores.

A new season had come. His own fields would be greening

156

up, rich with grain, if nothing happened to kill the crops. Areli knew from experience how close to the edge of disaster farmers lived. The first year of his marriage to Miriam, the harvest had been poor. It had taken two more years of good crops for him to break even, and now he had a chance to profit from his hard work.

His hands remembered: grubbing stones from his fields, chopping the weeds out from among the good plants, gathering the harvest in sheaves. Areli studied his scarred, rough hands. Some mornings he couldn't make them move properly. They were stiff and hurt too much. Through it all Miriam had worked beside him.

Certainly nothing came easily. The hard work had lined their faces, and Miriam had never been beautiful, as some folks counted it. But she was good—and strong—and Miriam believed in him. That mattered most.

Someday she would have fancy clothes, and they would have the money for celebrations and big weddings for their children—if they ever had children. Areli sighed. Three years, and no children. Miriam felt the shame of it more intensely than he did.

Others had noticed too. Jebediah, from the neighboring farm, had counseled him to put Miriam away and take another wife.

"What?" Areli snapped sharply, unable to hide his confusion.

The two men had been building a rock wall to divert water from the creek to their farms. Areli angrily shoved a rock into place and faced Jebediah.

"Miriam cannot give you sons or daughters. She is barren," Jebediah answered matter-of-factly. "The law gives you the right to—"

"No!" Areli interrupted, irritated by the suggestion. "The law cannot measure the love between a man and a woman."

"Maybe. But we're talking about your future. Without children, who will the farm go to? A stranger?"

Speaking evenly, emphasizing his words carefully, Areli responded. "I didn't marry Miriam for the children she could give me. I married her because I loved her, and I still do."

"But—"

"Enough! I will not waste my breath arguing. I will not send her away, no matter what the law says I can do. Come. There's work to do."

Through one of the windows Areli could see Miriam dancing with happy abandon. He smiled. He would rejoin her in a few moments, but he wanted to fill his lungs with the fresh air of the countryside and rest his mind.

The steward appeared suddenly from inside. He talked earnestly to an older woman. The tones of their conversation arrested Areli's attention.

"What do you mean there's no more wine, steward?" the woman asked.

"Forgive me, but it's true. The other servants just emptied the last skin."

"Then send someone quickly to buy more wine in the village."

"There isn't any to be found in Cana. That was the first thing I did. We purchased everything in town. What can we do?" the steward asked.

Without hesitation the woman responded, "Go and ask my Son to join me here. He is inside with the wedding party."

Areli recognized the woman then: Mary, recently widowed from Joseph, the carpenter of Nazareth. Neither Mary nor the wine steward had noticed Areli sitting quietly in the shadows. He knew that eavesdropping was hardly proper, but he couldn't think of a way to leave without attracting attention.

The steward returned quickly. Other servants trailed behind him. Following them closely walked a lone Man, Mary's Son, Jesus of Nazareth. Odd rumors had sprung up about Him recently. He had given up carpentry, sold His father's tools, and given the money to His mother to live on. Such an unexpected move drew the curious. Jesus had begun to gather disciples, establishing Himself as a teacher. It all seemed very strange. For the moment Areli felt caught up in the sheer presence of the Man.

"Hello, Mother. It's a beautiful wedding, isn't it?" Jesus smiled.

Areli could not miss the pride showing in Mary's eyes. She hugged Him fondly, ever a mother. "Weddings are one of the happiest times. Beginnings are always filled with the joys of hope."

"The steward said you wanted to see Me about something important. Is anything wrong?"

"They have no more wine, Son."

Jesus understood the implication immediately. Custom dictated that the host provide for his guests. A lack of wine, especially in an important celebration like a wedding, would demonstrate not only the host's unpreparedness but also might indicate a lack of hospitality.

"Dear woman," Jesus answered, cupping her chin in one strong hand, "why are you telling *Me* this? My time has not yet come."

Even as He spoke to His mother His attention strayed, oblivious to Mary's apology. Jesus' gaze fell on several large water jars used for ceremonial cleansings. At present they all stood as empty as Areli's wine cup. Mary noticed her Son's preoccupied manner and turned quickly to the steward. "Do whatever He tells you to do," she ordered.

"As you wish," the man replied, bowing slightly.

Mary squeezed her Son's hand as He stood silently looking at the water jars. He smiled down at her, obviously pleased with an idea that had come to Him. "Go back to the celebration, Mother, and don't worry about this. I will take care of it."

As Mary slipped away, Jesus ordered the servants to fill the jars with water from the well. They complied, though Areli noticed bewildered expressions on one or two faces. Areli could have slipped away then. Everyone seemed too busy to notice, but he found himself strangely intent on learning Jesus' solution to the problem.

The servants worked feverishly, knowing that soon a guest would discover the lack of wine. Jesus urged them on with quick, quiet words of encouragement. Finally each jar stood full, brimming with cold, clear well water. The servants stood back expectantly.

Jesus turned His face to the sky for a few moments, then moving quickly He dipped a finger into the water of each jar. Handing a serving vessel to the wine steward, Jesus said, "Draw from these jars and serve the master of the feast first."

The steward filled the vessel, carefully wiping the lip with a cloth. Even from a distance Areli could see the rich, dark-red stains on the once clean, white cloth! Astounded, the steward rushed off with the wine. Other servants followed, each carrying his own vessel of wine. Jesus headed toward the house.

Overcome with curiosity, Areli left his hidden nook and went to the jars. He filled his own wine cup with the deep red liquid, amazed at the miracle he had stumbled on.

"May I join you?"

Areli spun around, the wine in his cup sloshing over the rim. Jesus, a cup in His hand as well, stood near him.

"C-certainly," Areli managed to stammer.

Jesus seemed not to notice his discomfort but filled His own cup and raised it.

"What shall we toast?" Jesus asked.

"To life," Areli suggested, "and to the happiness of the newlyweds."

Jesus smiled, and they sipped the wine. The taste surprised Areli. It seemed to sparkle on his tongue. It was the taste of new wine—fresh and clean and full of life.

"I propose another toast to add to yours," Jesus said. A penetrating gleam lighted up His eyes. "To your children, and their children after them."

"But—" Areli began. Then he understood.

He lifted the cup and drank happily, long, and deep.

♦ ♦ ♦

# Good Intentions Are Not Enough

*Dan Fahrbach*

I JUST saw the top of her head over the hood of our Rabbit as she darted across the street. The driver of the silver Cadillac, coming through the red light a little late and a little too fast, couldn't have seen more than her skinny arms thrown up at the last instant. The point of the chrome bumper caught her in the ribs and carried her a few feet before her hands slid off the grille, and she disappeared.

Maybe the driver heard her tiny scream or felt a bump. Whatever, he braked to a stop beside us. Somewhere under his long car I knew there was a 3-year-old girl with braids that were too short and stuck straight out from her head.

I jumped out of our car and knelt to look under the Cadillac. But for a few seconds I couldn't open my eyes. I heard people yelling, and up the street an impatient driver honked his horn. When I finally looked, she was two feet away, very still. She looked unbroken.

A crowd gathered. The Cadillac backed away from the body, and a policeman straightened her legs as she began to cry. By the time the ambulance arrived she was screaming and trying to get away, to run, and it took two men to hold her down on the hot pavement. When they lifted her into the ambulance, I could see her braids were soaked with blood.

The ambulance whooped, and carried her away. It was only then that the policeman asked for her mother. The crowd looked around at each other. No one stepped forward. "What is her name? Doesn't anybody know who she is?" the policeman asked. "Where does she live?"

We could hear the last cries of the siren. The blood on the pavement already looked black.

"Terry's her brother." A youngster holding a soccer ball pointed up the street. A block away, we saw a child—maybe 5 years old—stumbling homeward, crying so hard he couldn't see.

At last, something we could do to help. My wife and I jumped in the car and drove up the street.

And help was needed. The mother did not have a car; she was too hysterical to drive anyway. But she needed to get to the hospital. We got her into the car and started driving in the direction the ambulance had gone. We were in a strange part of town, and when I asked her whether she knew the way to Children's Hospital, she pointed left. I turned. Two streets later she pointed left again, and again I turned. Then she pointed right. I should have noticed that something was wrong. She wasn't talking, or crying even—just trembling. But I was running red lights and stop signs, trying to get there fast. I thought her daughter was dying. Finally Kathryn leaned over from the back seat and told me the mother wasn't even watching where we were going. I looked, and Kathryn was right: the mother's eyes were closed, her head rocking back and forth.

I made one more turn, and we came to a stop in the parking

lot behind some abandoned apartments, lost.

It was as hard as anything I have ever done to stop the car, unfold the map, and look for Children's Hospital. Too many minutes passed before we found ourselves and started driving again.

Forty minutes later we arrived at the emergency room. Trika (her mother had begun to say her name over and over in the car) was in surgery. She had broken ribs, a punctured lung, and two broken legs. But she would be all right.

This happened months ago, last summer. But yesterday after I had lunch with a friend who told me he can no longer believe in God ("There is too much pain," he said. "Like constantly being run over by a truck."), I remembered Trika's accident. And I remember how badly I had wanted to help and how badly I had failed.

Good intentions come easily, but good intentions are not enough. Unless we know where we are and where we are going—unless we know the map—our solo efforts at being splendid neighbors and helpful friends are not likely to help much.

What is the map? The map involves a daily, earnest striving to know God. Through searching the Scriptures and prayer we become familiar with our context, our coordinates. Then it's not so easy to get lost.

Accidents are always surprises—even accidents of faith. But we do not have to be unprepared.

◆ ◆ ◆

# Bertie Harris, Mr. Stader, & Mrs. D.

## *Edwin Gallagher*

**B**ERTIE Harris' left eyelid was twitching. It always did that when he got excited. He was awfully embarrassed about it, and the more it twitched, the more embarrassed he became, and the more embarrassed he became, the more it twitched.

But on this occasion he needn't have worried. The two standing with him, Mr. Stader and Mrs. Deniliquin, appeared far too engrossed in their discussion to notice Bertie's twitching left eyelid.

"I have peace, peace, peace," declared Mrs. Deniliquin, "and you don't get that kind of peace from climbing Jacob's ladder."

"But Jacob strove with the Lord."

"Yes, Mr. Stader, and look at his reward—a broken thigh."

"Well, we all need to be humbled."

"Yes, but humility is primarily a gift. Love, purity, obedience, peace—all are gifts. Salvation is provided free; it's through grace, grace, grace."

Mrs. Deniliquin had an unsettling habit of repeating emphatic words three times. Bertie, who hadn't yet been able to say anything in the discussion, was glad she hadn't noticed his twitch, twitch, twitch.

"Mrs. D.," replied Mr. Stader [Mr. Stader had trouble pronouncing her name, so he just called her "Mrs. D."], "I realize it is all of grace, but we have a response to make—we are to strive to enter the strait gate, we must keep His commandments, work out our own salvation with fear and trembling, and show ourselves approved unto God. Faith without works is dead, dead, dead."

Mr. Stader had never in his life repeated his words like that. But he wished to show himself equal to Mrs. Deniliquin. He was by nature a shy man, his only obvious advantage over her being his height—he was six feet one and a half, but looked even taller than that because he was relatively thin. Mrs. Deniliquin, on the other hand, was five feet three in height, and appeared to be roughly the same in girth.

"Faith without works might be dead," she countered, "but works without faith are not just dead—they are moldy, rotten, rat-infested, and full of stench. Look at the Pharisees, look at the Galatians! Our works will come, once faith has accepted the work of Christ outside of us. Yes, the works will be there, but faith must be first, first, first."

"Well, I think—" tried Bertie, his eyelid twitching rapidly.

"I don't mean to interrupt," interrupted Mr. Stader, "but what did the Lord tell the members of the church at Ephesus? 'Repent, and do the works you did at first.' I agree with your main point, Mrs. D. We owe everything to Jesus; our works are detestable without Him. But it seems to me that you are leaving so many scriptures unexplained. Your attitude has me concerned. I'm not saying you're lost or anything, but I do fear your salvation could be in jeopardy."

"Well, Mr. Stader," replied Mrs. Deniliquin, drawing herself up and out to her full sixty-three inches, "I appreciate your concern for me, but my concern for you is even greater. There'll be no one passing through those pearly gates who doesn't have on the white garment. Don't you know it, there's not a thread of human works woven into it! Not a thread! Not a thread! Not a thread!"

Bertie Harris was now twitching wildly. A Christian of rich experience and deep understanding, he was just bursting with the thought that Jesus, who had both Mrs. Deniliquin and Mr. Stader in His hands, would no doubt be as happy to tolerate the variation in their thinking as He would be to tolerate the difference in their physique.

He was just about to say this, and Mrs. Deniliquin and Mr. Stader were both about to interrupt him, when there was a very loud noise and a long, bright flash of light—indeed, the noise was louder and the flash was longer and brighter than anything they had experienced before.

Later, sitting together in Levi Square, New Jerusalem, Mr.

Stader looked across at Mrs. Deniliquin and said, "Mrs. D., I'm glad your works were OK."

Mrs. Deniliquin laughed and replied, "Mr. Stader, I'm glad your faith was OK!"

Bertie, sitting nearby, was just about to say his piece about Jesus being happy to tolerate differences, when Mrs. Deniliquin looked over at him, smiled genuinely, and said, "And Bertie, we're *so* glad you lost your twitch."

◆ ◆ ◆

# Snow!

## *Charles Wilkinson*

FRED stuck his finger in my face. "You will never, never get these students to believe in snow. Oh, they'll listen to you, they'll even write it all down in their notebooks, but the whole time they'll be laughing at you behind your back because they know that the bit about snow and ice is 'White man's lies.' "

I was a little worried about Fred Pendergast. He was the science teacher at Rusangu Secondary School in Zambia, and he had been there a number of years. Maybe a few too many. I wasn't sure what was making him such a quitter. Perhaps he had been out in the sun too long. Or he was just getting tired. At any rate, such a defeatist attitude was unbecoming of a Christian missionary.

In sharp contrast, I was coming in fresh. Two months out of college, newly married, and ready to conquer the world, I was the school's new geography teacher. And I resolved not to show any impatience with Fred or anyone like him: I would simply inspire him to start trying again. I was sure my successes would be able to inspire anyone.

Fred wasn't done with me: "You might, if you really push it, get them to believe that *you* believe in snow. Once I got a whole group convinced that all Europeans believe in snow, including the ones at Cambridge who would be grading their tests. Then at least they would learn the basic facts about frozen precipitation."

"I'll get them to believe it themselves," I said calmly. Fred laughed at me.

After the first few weeks of settling in and getting started teaching, I selected my first group to learn about snow. They were the Form IVs (high school juniors). Not only were they the sharpest group in the school, but they had a unit coming up in geography on climate and weather.

We started with the obvious: the facts. I taught them all about the various types of precipitation: rain, sleet, hail, dew, frost, and snow. They believed me only when I talked about the wet ones.

Next I tried demonstration. I brought ice cubes from my refrigerator at home. There was a lot of laughing and shouting as the little blocks of ice were handed around the room. But the ice cubes didn't last long, and my hopes of convincing the class that day melted with them. It struck me that this was going to take some effort.

Thanksgiving came, and I still hadn't convinced anyone.

The rains came in December, and in that first rainy season I received a rare opportunity to show my students frozen precipitation: we got a hailstorm. It was the first hail in that area in more than 20 years, so none of the students had ever seen it before. It came while I was teaching another class, but I didn't let that slow me down. I took my Form II's running and yelling past the math room, where the Form IVs were, and to the consternation of the math teacher, they joined us in running out onto the soccer field. The hailstones were just big enough to hurt a little, and soon I had them picking up pieces and tasting them. I even convinced a few that it was the same stuff that had come out of my refrigerator. But the hot African sun followed the storm, and in almost no time the ice melted. As we slogged back to classes it was obvious that we had gotten wet for nothing.

But I wasn't about to admit defeat—not to Fred, anyway. The next unit in geography covered the properties of water, so I made my next try with that. They had learned from Mr. Pendergast in science class that water could change form, from liquid into steam or ice. But when I introduced the idea in geography, if was as though they had never heard it before.

"Hey, you know that!" I protested.

"But sir, we know that in science class, not geography class."

"Class dismissed!" I shouted, but before they got their hopes up, I added, "but you're not going anywhere. We are now going to have *science class.*"

I headed out the door, turned around, and entered the room again. They stood, as was their custom for starting a class, and the room fell silent.

"Good morning, class," I greeted.

"Good morning, sir," they echoed.

After I gave them permission to be seated, we launched into the properties of water, and it was amazing what they knew. It was an exciting educational experience correlating science and geography.

But alas, they didn't believe in snow in science class, and they didn't believe in it in geography class either, so when we combined the two, they still didn't believe in snow.

I finally gave up. It was awhile before I admitted it to Fred and the other teachers, but I finally did. Ron Schaffner, the English teacher, was sympathetic:

"Really, the difference is that in North America we experience both summer and winter every year, so we understand both the tropics and the polar regions. Out here in Africa, these people have never really seen winter."

Nearly two years later, shortly before returning to the States, I selected a ski film for a Saturday night program. I'd like to say that it was one last attempt to get them to believe in snow, but actually the reason was a little more personal: I wanted to see snow myself. I missed it. After living in the tropics for a while, I was beginning to wonder if I believed in snow anymore myself.

For that the film was very successful. It showed just about every ski slope in Europe and North America, and it made the Canadians especially homesick. The students enjoyed it too. Every time someone fell down, they cheered.

When the lights came on and the students were leaving, Benson Lusaka stopped me and wanted to talk. Benson had been in my old Form IV class, and had just finished secondary school. "Sir," he began, "I think I learned something from the film."

"Oh, do you believe in snow now?" I couldn't hide the excitement in my voice.

"No, I don't believe in snow, but I am willing to concede one point: it has to be a lot colder where that was filmed."

I looked at him, wondering how he could feel cold from a film.

"It was the clothes. Everyone had on much heavier clothing than they ever wear here. So it has to be colder." Benson had always been very fashion-conscious.

So I had to settle for that. One student admitting that it might be colder in the Northern Hemisphere than it is in the tropics. I was glad that teaching them about snow hadn't been my only objective.

The Schaffners were scheduled to return to the United States a few weeks before our return, so we did a lot of anticipating together. One afternoon we played a tape of organ music recorded in our old home church. The song that affected us the most was "A Song of Heaven and Homeland."

Then it was time for us to go back to the States. Only those who have lived overseas can fully appreciate the joy of returning to the home country. While my wife and I saw snow when we flew over the Alps (by moonlight), our first *American* snow was spotted from high over Newfoundland.

And then everything happened fast. There was a view of New York Harbor from 39,000 feet as we tried to spot the Statue of Liberty. There was the customs agent at Dulles Airport with a heavy American accent. There were relatives waiting.

That summer we took classes at Andrews University, in Michigan, and that September we moved to Detroit. One day in autumn I had a committee meeting at Andrews University. When I went to the cafeteria for lunch, I got a real surprise. I ran into Benson Lusaka! After a long African handshake we hugged each other. Benson was the first Zambian I had seen in months, and he seemed just as happy to see me. We had only a few minutes to talk, and we spent most of it talking about Zambia. I realized for the first time that I was missing Africa a little, but Benson was missing it desperately.

As our paths split, he going to a class and me heading back to the meeting, he finally brought it up.

"You were sure right about the cold winters here in America, but I haven't seen any of the snow you talked about." A gentle breeze blew a few newly fallen leaves past us, but the October sun felt warm.

"How long are you going to be here at Andrews?" I asked.

"I have a two-year visa, but I hope to stay longer."

"Then you'll see some snow," I smiled. "You'll know it when you see it."

We did another African handshake and parted. I had just added another reason to look forward to that first snowfall.

My next visit to Andrews University was in January. After going through the cafeteria line, I wandered around a bit in the dining area, looking for Benson. Not finding him, I sat down at one of the small tables by the windows.

Outside it was bleak. There was twice as much snow in western Michigan as there was in Detroit, and I had thought it was bad in Detroit. We were getting a mild winter, the weathermen were telling us, but my thin blood didn't see it that way. Because the winter was "mild" Lake Michigan hadn't frozen, so they had gotten a lot of "lake effect" snow. At least that's how they explained it to me when I asked why snow was falling out of a blue sky. Looking down on the campus from the cafeteria, the many sidewalks looked like some psychologist's maze.

Suddenly Benson was beside me. Again the greeting was warm. We sat down together at the little table, and I waited impatiently for him to finish praying.

"Ah, Benson, what do you see out the window?" I pointed with my thumb.

"I believe!" he shouted. "I believe!"

But Benson didn't want to talk about snow; he wanted to talk about Zambia. He was still homesick. So we talked about Rusangu, we talked about friends, we talked about where it was warm. It didn't take him long to get me missing it too.

When we finished eating, I offered him a ride the short distance to Meier Hall, the men's dorm. It gave us a few more minutes to talk.

"I'm writing to all the boys in our class and telling them about the snow. They should know that you were right."

"They won't believe you. They'll say that I bewitched you."

Benson stared at my hands, which I was flexing to keep from freezing to the steering wheel. He kept his breath down and off the windshield. We talked some more about Zambia in January: summer, rainy season, everyone wearing short pants.

"You're right," he said as we pulled up to the back of Meier

Hall, as close as I could get to the door. "No one there is going to believe me."

He opened the car door and made ready for a rush through the blowing snow.

"What we have to do," he said through clenched teeth, "is bring them over here and show them."

◆ ◆ ◆

# The War Is Over

## D. N. Marshall

TIME was, and not so long ago, I rode a ferry home twice each semester. The ferry service in this British port city, however, was unreliable. I spent many luggage-encumbered hours by the gangway, peering into the fog for the appearance of the familiar paddle steamer. These hours gave me more opportunity than I welcomed to take in the salt spray, the ozone, and the atmosphere.

By the gangway was a sea-shaken brick-built shelter. Around it slunk the city's human jetsam, who looked as if they might disconnect my freckles for the price of a whiskey. Within this shelter sat one solitary man. *Always the same man.* Rain, shine, snow, or blow he was there.

On wild winter nights when the ocean's salt flood threatened to sweep his shelter out to sea, he was there. On bitterly cold mornings when frost covered the railings, he was there. On balmy summer evenings, moon dry, silent, and airless, the shadows black without shading, he was there.

He was in late middle age, tall, and dressed in a shabby raincoat. His eyes were always fixed on the horizon. What was he looking for? Why was he there? Deep unhappiness was engraved on that face. And something more indefinable, ghastly.

One day in late summer when tides were unusually low, I munched on a frozen sandwich and sat on an outdoor seat. My mind was full of Calvin, Bunyan, and Baxter while thunder rolled and reverberated over hills of cloud.

"They're coppin' it at Dunkirk." In my preoccupation I had been aware that a presence had settled down beside me. I was now only too aware that it had a voice. *It was him.*

The first scatters of rain were beginning to fall, and I made my move for shelter, but he followed me.

"You got back all right then? So did I. There was bombs and shells and bullets. Don't know how we made it but we did . . . Got back home . . . whole street bombed out . . . our house, a direct hit . . . wife and kids gone, mother buried alive . . . George and Frank, me brothers, still in the thick of the shindy. . . expectin' 'em back . . . This might be them now."

As the ferry disgorged its human cargo—vacationers, shoppers, commuters—he searched the face of every man in the crowd pouring through the barrier, looking for the features of George and Frank . . .

How many times had he gone through this ritual? How many times had that look of abject disappointment set in? What kept alive the hope that two long-lost brothers would return? Where did he spend his nights? Who fed him?

In the earnestness of youth, and before I realized that he sensed and thought and experienced but did not hear, I tried to tell him, *The war is over.* It had been over for decades. Dunkirk had receded into history.

He couldn't hear me.

All that filled his ears was the sound of shells thundering, bullets whining, voices calling frantically.

The war was over. But not in *his* head.

"Then he came and told those who were far from God and us who were near to Him that the war was over" (see Ephesians 2:17).

Through the Shepherd this life is not a downward spiral to destruction, a treadmill to oblivion. It is an upward way to freedom. It is a hope, live, burning, inextinguishable, in all experiences. It is a joy that none can take from you. It is love that serves and is catching. It is a peace that is lasting. It is unity and reconciliation, oneness.

Through Jesus the war is over.

But it lives on in the minds of some. The bullets still whine.

The shells still rumble. The walls, the barriers that divide and enclose, are still there. The treadmill is still in motion. The battle to earn what is beyond our power to earn, to deserve what is beyond our merits, rages, and takes its toll in those who fall by the wayside, unable to continue the fight.

Many have tried the religion of Jesus and found it difficult. And they have found it difficult because they have failed to grasp the first essential of the gospel: *The war is over*. It was won at the cross on a green hill.

♦ ♦ ♦

# Zorb

## *Don Watson with Shirley Kroman*

ZORB. Don't ask me why I decided to call it that. The name isn't important anyway. It's just that I wanted to name it something, and Zorb somehow came to my mind when I thought about having to die, and hellfire, and such. But first, let me explain.

You see, I wasn't sure God had considered all the alternatives in how to get rid of sinners. Why do sinners have to die, anyway?

Oh, I know the Bible says the wages of sin is death, but *that's* not a reason. *Why* are the wages death?

I've also considered the philosophy that God kills no one. People separate themselves from Him, the Source of life. If one separates himself from life, he dies as surely as a refrigerator defrosts if unplugged. However, countless people have separated themselves from God, yet they do not dissolve, disintegrate, or die off immediately because of their separation. The devil has lived on after separation. Evidently God sustains them for now in some way. Why is God opposed to continuing the same plan eternally?

Which brought me to my own very thoughtful alternative to the ultimate cleansing of hellfire. Obviously God doesn't want the righteous to be constantly exposed to the evil of the wicked. And, of course, we mustn't forget that the wicked themselves would be miserable in the holy atmosphere of heaven. So the two groups certainly could not cohabit there.

*But what about an isolation ward?* That's when I thought of Zorb—a big planet somewhere on the very edge of God's universe where the wicked can do exactly as they please.

Why couldn't God grant sinners eternal life on this isolation planet? They wouldn't have to depend on God; they could be responsible for their own actions. Live the way *they* want to live. Those who chose not to depend on God would be isolated so they couldn't contaminate the righteous.

Sound good? I thought so, so I let my imagination travel to Zorb. Come with me for a few moments.

Your neighbor on Planet Zorb, James Bondowski, just bought a Mazda RX-7. Problem is, you have a Lamborghini and he decides he prefers that. "George, I want your car. Give me your keys," he demands.

"No way, man," you reply.

"I said, the keys," he responds.

"Forget it, Bondowski," you say as you excuse yourself. But soon you find that Bondowski is extremely serious. He pushes a button on the bottom of his shoe and a knife shoots out the toe. Using a succession of karate kicks, he stabs you again and again, causing excruciating pain. Writhing in agony, you long to die, but you can't. You have eternal life!

Old Tim Cornway has been smoking for 3,422 years. He has a tremendous case of emphysema. Every word spoken causes agony, and each moment is a fight for life. He begs to die. But he can't. He has eternal life!

Tom Sellout contracted skin cancer 1,200 years ago, and now open sores and ulcers cover his entire body. He can't sit or lie down. He's in constant pain and would welcome death, but he can't die. He has eternal life!

Joan Call-ins has been totally rejected by her 12 husbands and beaten by the last three. Her children, abused and brimming over with hate, scream curses of contempt at her. Repeatedly she has attempted suicide, but with no success. You see, she has eternal life!

Eventually every man, woman, and child on overpopulated, polluted, infested, infected, diseased Zorb would be in excruciating pain—emotionally, mentally, and physically. They would scream for death, but they cannot die. They have eternal life!

In our mind's flight to Zorb we have seen what it really would be—a planet of eternal torment. God allows death to come as a *kindness,* lest Planet Earth become Planet Zorb.

A God of love can't let sin torture people forever, any more than He could burn people forever. The Bible presents God in mercy, making an end to all pain. "For, behold, the day cometh, that shall burn as an oven; and all the proud, yea, and all that do wickedly, shall be stubble: and the day that cometh shall burn them up, saith the Lord of hosts" (Malachi 4:1).*

The good news of the gospel is that no one need die or live on Planet Zorb. The Bible, history, and common sense make it abundantly clear that sin maims, tortures, and eventually destroys us. Through no choice of our own this sin was passed down to us. But on the cross of Calvary, God's Son paid our death debt and gave us back the choice.

Sin, not God, is killing us. God so loved us that He gave His only Son that whoever believes in Him won't be eternally destroyed by sin but will have everlasting life.

Without Christ there would have been no choice—there would have been only death. Sin would kill us. Now we have a choice.

So why would you want to die?—unless you were on Planet Zorb.

---

* For more on this, see *The Fire That Consumes* by Edward Fudge, published by Providential Press.

◆ ◆ ◆

# Lot's Wife Remembers

## *Deborah Anfenson-Vance*

SODOM wasn't perfect, but it was home," she said. "People misjudge me. But if you want to be fair, you must not say 'Lot's wife loved Sodom,' because God knows there were things about that place that I hated. No, you must say, 'Lot's wife loved her home.' That would be the truth.

"Of course, it was more than that. What is it, I ask you, that makes any of us return to even the most unpleasant of homes? It is security. Predictability. Knowing which chair to sit in, how soft (or hard) the mattress, where the roof leaks, in what place the water jug is kept. Knowing who will sling the insult (and how much he will mean it), who will pay the compliment, who will be the boss. Home is knowing. Home is the world, ordered as we would order it. And leaving home is to destroy that world.

"So when the men came with news about Sodom, it was as if they had announced the end of all things. 'The whole earth will disintegrate tomorrow morning,' they could have said, and it would have made no difference to me. I could see no life beyond Sodom. It had become my home, my life.

"And it was like losing my life to close the door that one last time and to walk away. Did I say *walk?* No, we were dragged away. There was no time for me to think of what we were leaving, only time to feel it in my heart. And as we ran, farther and farther from the place of our home, they came like an army sent to take us back. An army of a thousand happy memories. Family meals, the baby's first steps, guests entertained, secrets shared at the marketplace. Cool nights around the fire, warm evenings on the balcony. Memories. I would have wept tears of blood to make those memories live again. We were comfortable; we were happy. Never again would we find such happiness, I was sure. So in the end, I refused to let go.

"When in your mind you see me turn my head for that last fatal look, do not expect the painted lips, the hard eyes worn by women of the world. No, see instead the sadness of a refugee, the face of a mother whose last vision is not of a Sodom in flames but of a home on fire. Destroyed. The bed on which my husband loved me. The room where our babies were born. The earth in which my kinsmen sleep. See me, and know that what I longed for was home. Understand that what I wanted was good. That what I wanted is what you want.

"Like you, I wanted heaven. But I wanted it too soon. And it came out like a cake unbaked, like a sour apple, like a child born too early.

"So what is my sin? you wonder. What is wrong with home? you ask. I will tell you the last answer first, and that is Nothing. As for my sin, it is an understandable one. I wanted what was good for a while to be good forever. I had no wish for anything new, that is, for anything truly new. Oh yes, new bread, fresh water, maybe even a new dress or a new baby. But I did not want new thoughts or a new life, new opinions, or a new way of looking at the world. And so I became what you see today—a pillar of stagnant goodness, a monument to the past.

"If it is possible for me to say a few more words, I would like to tell you what I learned too late—that to live is to change. That to be truly alive is to be every day newborn, to experience God's universe as if at any time anything could happen. To be ready to lay down the good thing in your hand in order to pick up the better thing lying at your feet.

"I will also tell you that to have home you must be willing to leave home. For all of life is about leaving and coming and finding home and discovering new homes. When you leave your parents to go to school. When you leave school to go to a job. When you leave misconceptions to search for truth. Yes, life is about leaving. One day you will be asked to walk away from what is yours, and if you do, you will find something that no one can take away from you. If you do not, you will become like me—a form with no life.

"Here is a saying that did not come about in my lifetime, but after. Listen. 'Whoever seeks to gain his life will lose it, but whoever loses his life will preserve it.' Think about these words. And remember me."

◆ ◆ ◆

# River of Life, Pool of Death

## *Jim Robertson*

THEY were obviously trapped, doomed to a slow, suffocating death. They had taken refuge in a small pool, a back eddy of Eagle Creek when it had been highest during the late spring runoff. Since then the stream level had dropped, and a sandbar prevented them from returning to the stream.

The young steelhead and salmon, no larger than minnows, would never have a chance to grow, swim downstream, and become great fish in the Pacific Ocean. The Columbia, Willamette, and Clackamas rivers, and eventually Eagle Creek itself, would never see these fish fight their way back against the current to perpetuate their kind.

I had been seeking early summer trout, but seeing the plight of these tiny fish, I leaned my fly rod against a tree, hung my fishing vest on a branch, and set about to rescue them.

Already the water in their pool was becoming stale and accumulating a slight scum on the surface. *If I had a shovel,* I thought, *I could easily dig a channel through the sandbar and set them free. The escaping water would carry them out.*

Sloshing around in my hip waders, I used my hands, the closest thing to a shovel I had, to dig a channel. It was hard work, for the stream had mixed sticks and debris with the sand. When I did get a small channel opened, the flowing water quickly cut into the sandy sides, causing them to slough off into the stream and make it shallow.

I kept working until I got a fair-sized channel opened and then stood back to watch the fish flow out—but no fish flowed out.

The fingerlings had fled to the other side of the pool and were schooling, hiding in the leaves near the debris-choked edges. I tried chasing them in the direction of the outlet as a cowboy would herd cows, but the tiny fish carefully avoided the stream that would mean life to them. Two or three did get near the outlet, but upon sensing the flow of water, they innately turned upstream and swam back into the pool.

Since there was no one else around, I puzzled aloud, "Fish, can't you see that I'm trying to *save* you?" But they could neither hear nor understand me. I thought about how an incarnation (inichthyation?) might help the situation. I could become one of them, communicate however fish communicate with one another, and show them that to do what doesn't come naturally (in this case, swimming downstream) would result in their freedom and life. But I couldn't do that.

I decided a discarded bait container left by a littering fisherman might help scoop these creatures to freedom. A search up and down the stream revealed no containers that day.

Finally, with cupped hands I waded carefully around the little pool catching one at a time and tossing it into the main stream. As I held the tiny fish in the palm of my hand I marveled at the distinct markings of their salmonoid heritage—the midline reddish stripe and orange-tinted fins so delicate and almost transparent.

The smaller, slow ones were the easiest to catch, but even then the scoop-from-behind technique was required for any kind of success. I tossed each one from its handful of water over the sandbar into the river of freedom. Some probably would become the prey of larger fish, but at least now they had a chance of surviving and becoming 10- to 12-pounders.

The bigger ones were faster and had no intention of being rescued. I could imagine them saying to me as they darted out of my hands, "Get lost, fisherman. I like this pool and can take care of myself. I don't need your help. I'll become a great fish on my own. See how much bigger than the others I am already?"

"Ah, fish," I'd reply, "you have no idea of your potential, of how great a fish you really can be. But, alas, you won't let me save you."

Altogether I was able to scoop up four or five dozen and release them to the living part of the stream. The rest were too hard to catch. I had to leave them to their "freedom."

Picking up my vest and rod, I took a last look at the channel I had dug. I was amazed to see a tiny fish I had rescued starting to work its way from the river back to the stagnant pool. After shooing it downstream, I kicked in the sides of the channel to close it. I didn't want those I had freed going back, even if it meant permanently sealing in those that remained in the pool.

As I hiked the trail back to the truck, I pondered hard the rescue efforts of the original Fisherman.

◆ ◆ ◆

# Get Out in the Name of Jesus

## *Steven Mosley*

I T all started with David's brushing his teeth. Ordinarily that's not a very subversive activity, but in this case the boy was looking for trouble.

Rest period during a week euphemistically labeled "Opportunity Camp" was an hour in which we cabin counselors tried to infuse an utterly alien tranquillity into the throbbing spirits and bodies of our adolescent campers. Each of us attempted to control eight feisty kids who had been bused down from Chicago ghettos for a dose of communion with nature. Constant efforts to keep Whites and Blacks from fighting left me drained by the end of the day. Opportunity Camp was an intense strain, but it proved to be one of the most worthwhile struggles of my life.

David had been particularly rebellious that day. A couple of fights, food splattered in the cafeteria, late for every roll call—his record of misbehavior grew by the hour. So I restricted him to the cabin during rest period. No going down to the bathroom to goof off this time. No throwing rocks through the screens of other cabins on the way.

David and I had been having our confrontations from the start. He was a kid big enough to be on his own; I was an adult pressing my weight down. His passions were already deep and hard. I sensed, or guessed, that behind his chafing snarl he longed for the discipline he outwardly hated. What was his home like? All I had were impressions from sociology statistics and the six o'clock news.

But David could also say genial prayers with me when the cool of the night shut out the day's battles and suggested an intimate Lord. We had our good times together. He displayed a fresh exuberance learning to swim in the lake. A part of him wanted to breathe in the green. Another part labored under a shadow, the imprint of what children must endure growing up in the hands of sinners who don't know that they are.

That afternoon I looked over from my mediatorial cot in the middle of the cabin and observed David on his bed sullenly, furiously brushing his teeth. Taking up the challenge, I said, "I told you you're not going to the bathroom." David kept brushing and frothing, and then, staring at me inscrutably, spit on the cement floor. I did not speak kindly. "You'd better not do that again."

David kept brushing and spit again. Indignation rushed up my spine. Grabbing the boy, I lifted him from his bed and laid him down hard on the cement. I rubbed his body on the floor, wiping the spittle with his many-colored striped shirt.

David exploded too. Crying and screaming, he wrenched loose from my hands and threw himself against his bed. Something broke open inside, and an acidic rage cut at his face. After a few moments of aimless frenzy he started flinging his clothes into his suitcase. Between sobs he shouted something about "going home; can't take no more."

I regretted losing my temper and tried to calm David down. What would the camp director think if the kid ran screaming down to the office? My words of urgent comfort were drowned. David's arms flailed against the pinewood.

Five minutes. No letting up. I decided to get the boy away from the other kids, and dragged him, moaning and kicking, all the way to the bathroom.

Isolated inside the cool cinderblock building, I was sure he would spend his rage. But it grew. His rough cries looked for a climax, a way out, but could find none.

My fear grew too. I tried to hold David, but he flung himself against me, trying to get away, tears rolling, nose running, mouth frothing with toothpaste. I pushed him back from the doorway again and again. Twenty minutes. These temper tantrums are supposed to end, aren't they?

In my desperation I used difficult words. "I love you, David. I want to help you." He could not hear, sealed airtight in his blazing emotion. All the lackings and longings of a cramped soul flared at me, screaming at the oppression.

Finally, after a fierce, helpless shove, David threw himself on the floor. He lay at my feet frothing and writhing, passion unabated. It was then that those old tales hit me, those ancient tales people squirm over uncomfortably, primitive word-of-mouth tales about something that is never supposed to happen in times like ours. I saw flashes of Jesus on the field of battle, facing a naked, militant evil.

Reaching down, I picked up David by the shoulders. He stood facing away from me. A bit self-conscious and very desperate, I said, "Get out in the name of Jesus." Twice. I didn't sound to myself like one wielding the solid, sure wedge of authority. It was just a clean fling of faith. David couldn't hear me, he was still screaming so loudly. But I was, tentatively perhaps, addressing a third party.

And he stopped. Two or three seconds after my impulsive command he was supple in my hands, sobbing softly. I led him over to a washbasin and ran water into it. He let me wash off the tears, mucus, toothpaste, and spittle smeared on his face.

"You feel better?" I asked, earnest and awed.

"I'm sorry." He whimpered like a son made tender toward his father. "I'm sorry." Strange words from David's mouth.

I led the boy over to a shower stall, and we sat down amid the graffiti. David was gentle under my arm for those few moments — malleable. And I tried to explain what was only beginning to dawn on me in full measure. "There is a wild passion that can run over us, David — something stronger than us. But Jesus wants to put His peace in our hearts. Jesus is the one who made you calm. He made you feel better. He wants to make you strong in a different way, David."

I don't really understand the exact mechanics involved in demonic activity. There may very well be a term in a psychology textbook for David's emotional seizure. But I am more interested in solutions than in labels. To me the difference between losing your temper and wrestling with a demon is basically one of degree, not substance. We are all struggling against demonic forces, whatever their manifestation, and the activity of Christ is what gets results. That's what matters.

I wish I could say that the godly spell cast in that summer camp bathroom produced a lasting peace, that David became a saint by proclamation. But we had more battles before Opportunity Camp was over. His anger was deeper and wider than I could then encompass.

I will never forget David's hard face staring from a window in the Chicago-bound train. He did not wave back.

But when I pray for him now, my hopes are buoyed by the memory of that liberating name. That scrappy deliverance during rest period was only spiritual first aid, but it carries a promise that Jesus's present Spirit provides resources to match all the forces arrayed against David. There is a love big enough to swallow up his raging scars. However trapped David may be in a doomed environment, Christ offers him—and all of us—complete healing.

◆ ◆ ◆

# All the Way Back

## C. V. *Garnett*

A HOT, sticky night in Miami. Brad could feel the heat rising from the sidewalk as he ambled down Biscayne Boulevard. Cars whizzed past, people walked past, sirens wailed past. Brad did not feel a part. He wanted, in fact, to be *apart*. By himself. If only he could be alone—to pray aloud.

Sometimes silent prayer will not do. There are times when a man needs to hear the sound of his own voice reverberating to God. *If only there was a wayside chapel,* Brad thought, *or a church that was open.*

He walked on another two blocks. Then he saw it. He could

hardly believe it, but there it was. A lovely glass door opened into a dimly lit chapel. Small wooden pews, a tiny altar, soft lighting. Perfect. Next to the door hung a sign: "Come in, you are welcome to sit, pray, meditate, or eat your lunch."

Brad noticed by the entrance a podium holding a guest book. A delightful idea. The book had columns for names, addresses, and comments. People from numerous states had autographed the book. In the comment column some had written evangelical statements: "Praise the Lord" or "Jesus saves" or "I have found Him!" Many expressed appreciation for the very existence of such a place. Brad wrote a note expressing his good fortune in finding this wayside chapel.

Then the page blew back, and one statement caught his eye. In neat penmanship were written these poignant words: "Nancy was here and left for good."

A pathetic statement. At best a flippant, feeble joke. At worst the sincere and desperate declaration of a soul. Either way, Brad thought it tragic, for it revealed a girl who was disillusioned. It was an expression of rejection of God.

The words stung Brad. So much so that when he seated himself in the rough-hewn pew he could think of nothing else. His own problems took a back seat to Nancy's.

Who was this girl? Why did she write such a thing? Only God knew.

The prayers Brad had longed to pray for himself were superseded. Nancy and her soul became his only concern. Kneeling in the dimly lit chapel, he lifted her to God in prayer. Prayed that God might reach down, reach out, reach in, and save her.

Rising from his knees, Brad felt unburdened, as if some mighty hand had lifted a heavy beam from his shoulders. Brad remembered reading somewhere that intercessory prayer is a perfume whose fragrance blesses twice—the one who touches it and the one touched by it.

With reluctance Brad left the little chapel. He had found a needed haven and, in that place, a peace. He began his walk toward home.

He was only a few blocks from the chapel when an inspiration struck him.

He turned around and began running. He ran all the way back.

Nancy would hardly be there tonight. She had, after all, written that she would *never* return. Still she might come back sometime. The Spirit of the Lord could, in answer to Brad's own prayer, call her back for an unscheduled visit. And if so, she must know that someone cared. That God indeed cared.

Breathless, Brad opened the glass door and stepped inside the chapel. It was still empty. He turned to the visitors' book and picked up the pen. In the column beside the words "Nancy was here and left for good" he wrote:

"God was here and left for Nancy."

◆ ◆ ◆

# You Can't Kill Me!

## *Stanley Maxwell*

THIS *true story reveals how during the Cultural Revolution in China some Christians still practiced their beliefs in God. Mr. Wong (a pseudonym) now lives in southern China.*

"Do you know my friend Jesus?" Mr. Wong often asked.

To some people this question seemed out of place for two reasons: First, Mr. Wong was a Chinese expressing his personal feelings about a friend (something seldom done by Chinese). And second, he was expressing his feelings about Jesus in Communist China at a time when talking about anyone besides Party Chairman Mao Zedong could result in a prison term or even a bullet to the head.

Persuading people to believe in Jesus (or proselytizing, as the Communists called it) was illegal in China and still is today. So Mr. Wong's question "Do you know my friend Jesus?" was daring indeed.

Yet the 60-some-year-old Mr. Wong persisted in asking his

question every day of everyone he met. It didn't seem to matter to him that China was in the midst of the Cultural Revolution, and that people were being arrested and killed every day by the government's youthful Red Guards.

Mr. Wong just wanted everyone to know his friend Jesus. He wasn't worried that someone might report him. But someone must have reported him, for one day Mr. Wong was visited by blue-clad youths with red arm bands. He was expecting them.

"We hear you've been talking about your friend Jesus," they snapped.

"Yes, I have," Mr. Wong replied, recognizing these youths in Sun Yat-sen jackets as members of the notorious Red Guard. "Do *you* know my friend Jesus?"

"Stop it!" the Red Guards commanded. "Don't you know it's illegal to talk about Jesus? Marx says religion is the opium of the people. It's time you were liberated from all this feudalistic nonsense and came into step with New China. Wake up and see the foolishness of all your bourgeois liberalism and Western ideas. You must follow the sayings in the little red book of our great leader, Mao Zedong."

"I cannot," Mr. Wong replied.

"You won't stop your counterrevolutionary activities?" the Red Guard shouted.

"I cannot stop talking about my friend Jesus, if that's what you mean." Mr. Wong spoke calmly. "Jesus is my best friend, and He can be your friend, too."

"We have a law!" the Red Guard barked.

"I know the law."

"You know the law! And do you know what we do to people who break the law?"

"I know."

"We take them to prison!"

"I'm ready. My things are packed." Mr. Wong picked up his case of meager belongings. "Take me!"

"Good! Maybe in prison you can be reeducated to abandon the error of your ways. Maybe in prison you will come to recognize the correctness of the people's party. We won't tolerate counterrevolutionaries. The people's revolution must go forward. You are a counterrevolutionary! Men! The dunce cap!"

A Red Guard jumped at the leader's command, crammed a

paper dunce cap on Mr. Wong's head, and shoved him out the door onto the dusty streets.

Another of the guards held Mr. Wong's head down as they walked. The Red Guards formed a procession marching down the dirty streets past the endless throngs, and they chanted Mr. Wong's crimes to the masses. Word of Mr. Wong's arrest had spread widely by the time the Red Guards paraded him into the prison yard.

But if the Red Guards thought they could silence Mr. Wong by placing him behind bars, they were mistaken. In prison he found many inmates willing to know his friend Jesus and to talk about Jesus with him.

Angrily the guards in the prison called him in for interrogation. They thought it time to teach him a lesson.

"Do you know why you're here, Mr. Wong?"

"For talking about my friend Jesus," Mr. Wong replied.

"That's right. Why are you still talking about Him? Don't you know it's forbidden to talk about Jesus in China?"

"Yes, I know."

"Then are you going to stop?"

"No. I cannot stop talking about my friend. Lonely prisoners need to know Jesus. It's my duty."

"It's your duty to study and obey the correct sayings of Chairman Mao in his little red book. You should study Mao's sayings with the other prisoners. Do you know what will happen to you if you don't stop talking this superstitious bourgeois liberalism?"

"No," Mr. Wong acknowledged.

"We'll throw you into a stricter prison!"

"That's fine," Mr. Wong said. "I'm not afraid. I'll still talk about my friend Jesus wherever you put me."

"Then we'll take you away!" the guard shouted.

"Take me. I'm ready."

The guards noticed that Mr. Wong's bag was already packed.

They transferred him into a stricter prison. But here too he asked the prisoners if they knew his friend Jesus. And soon there were a number who talked about Jesus with him. The guards responsible for Mr. Wong's re-education became angrier than ever. So they decided it was time to teach him a lesson he could never forget.

"Do you know why you're here?" they asked him.

"Yes."

"Why?"

"Because I talk about my friend Jesus."

"Correct. Don't you know it's illegal to talk about Jesus?"

"Yes."

"Are you going to stop this feudalistic superstition?" The guard stared into Mr. Wong's eyes.

"I can't stop talking about Jesus."

"You won't stop?"

"No."

"You have to! We have a law!" The guard's commanding tone could have galvanized the dead.

"You can't stop me."

"Is that what you think? Do you know what we'll do to you if you don't stop talking this bourgeois liberalism?"

The guard examined Mr. Wong's dossier for something he could use. His finger hit upon a line, and a rare smile spread across his face. "You're a troublemaker. You've been transferred once already. We must teach ruffians like you a lesson. We'll transfer you again to Qinghai hard labor camp. There we shall see if we can't liberate you from all this religious opiate you so stubbornly cling to. It's people like you who hold back the progress of the people's rightful and benevolent dictatorship."

Mr. Wong gulped but mustered a brave "Take me. I'm ready." He picked up his packed bag and followed the guards.

Anyone sent on the long road to Qinghai in the Cultural Revolution felt pangs of dread, for it was a place you could check into but never leave. Mr. Wong wondered if God would protect him as He did Daniel, or let him die, as He did Stephen.

Qinghai is a barren, flat land with hard ruddy soil and clumps of green grass. One of the main reasons prisoners didn't return from Qinghai was that the grass growing there was poisonous. The prison guards rationed so little food to the inmates and worked them so hard that to fend off starvation many tried eating the grass. Then they died of poisoning.

If anyone tried to escape, there was nowhere to go. The prisoner could easily be found on the flat terrain. Besides, the weather in Qinghai is windy year-round, unbearably cold at night even in summer, and bitterly cold in the winter. And if the wind or cold didn't wear out an escaping prisoner, the thin air would.

Mr. Wong had not met anyone released from Qinghai yet. He didn't expect to be released, nor did he plan to escape. But he knew he didn't have to be afraid, for God was with him.

The guards escorted him to a room for indoctrination.

"Do you know why you're here?" The questioning was beginning to sound like a broken record.

"Because I talk about my friend Jesus." He answered as patiently as before.

"You can't talk about Him."

"I know."

"Are you going to quit?"

"No, I cannot."

"Do you know what we'll do to you if you don't quit?"

"What can you do? You can't kill me!" Mr. Wong himself couldn't believe what he heard himself express. Why had he said those words?

The guards' eyes glared. They looked at each other, then nodded. *This old man is challenging us,* they thought. *Who is he to say we can't kill him?* Mentally they rubbed their hands together.

They took Mr. Wong into another room and administered a form of Qing Dynasty torture. The guards tied Mr. Wong's arms behind his back. Then they tied a rope to the roof and hung him by his arms. They placed a millstone around his neck to make him heavier. Then they threw scoops of gravel at him off and on.

At the end of the working day the guard asked, "Are you ready to quit talking this Jesus nonsense?"

Mr. Wong was in such pain; he longed to have his feet firmly planted on the floor again. His arms felt like they would rip from his shoulder blades. He was bruised and bleeding all over, and especially on his face. The stench of fresh and dried blood dulled his senses. The pain he was suffering screamed at him to say yes, he would quit. He even thought he would *have* to give in—but not today. Tomorrow, maybe, but for the sake of his friend Jesus, no! not today.

"No. I cannot stop talking about my friend Jesus." Mr. Wong thought his voice sounded disconnected from himself.

The guards left him hanging.

The next day the guards again entered Mr. Wong's cell. Again they threw shovelful after shovelful of sharp rocks against his body and asked him the same question: "Will you stop talking your Jesus nonsense?"

The pain was much worse the second day. His body bled easier because the rocks reopened yesterday's scabs. The scabs that remained itched, but he couldn't scratch them. Now his body odors combined with the excessive carbon dioxide in the cell to make him feel faint. Mr. Wong began to feel detached from his body. *Oh, to be on firm ground instead of swinging from the room.* Again he was tempted to say yes, but no—tomorrow, yes, maybe he should tomorrow, but for Christ's sake, not today.

"No," he again heard himself say, "I cannot stop talking about my friend Jesus." Again the guard left him hanging.

The guards re-entered his cell every day for a week. Each time they continued the torture and asked him the same question. And each time Mr. Wong felt the same temptation but gave the same answer.

On the seventh day they thought he was dead, so they took him down and threw him on the dead pile. Some time later Mr. Wong came to and found himself prostrate atop hundreds of stinking, decaying bodies. He crawled off the dead pile and into the camp—to the astonishment of the other inmates and the embarrassment of the guard. *They had not been able to kill him!*

For the time being the guards thought it best to leave him alone. When Mr. Wong entered the camp, his face and body were covered with scabs from the torture. But amazingly soon his skin was clear and healthy again, and all pain in his arms and back vanished. The scabs flaked off easily, and his skin softened. No scars remained. Mr. Wong thanked his friend Jesus for healing him miraculously.

Again Mr. Wong began asking his fellow inmates, "Do you know my friend Jesus?" Many were interested in talking with him about Jesus, and soon he had a group of followers who liked to talk about their friend Jesus.

Frustrated, the guards decided it was time to teach him a real lesson. The guards took Mr. Wong into a cell. "Do you know why you are here?"

"Yes. It's because I like to talk about my friend Jesus," Mr. Wong said confidently. "He can be your friend, too."

"Shut up!" The prison guard barked.

Mr. Wong stopped talking.

"You know you can't talk about this Jesus. It's against the law."

"I know."

"Are you going to stop?"

"If Chairman Mao himself were standing here asking me the same question, I would still say I cannot stop talking about my friend Jesus."

Infuriated, the guards seized the 60-some-year-old Wong. They viciously broke both his arms and both his legs, then threw him out onto the dead pile again.

Mr. Wong walked back into the camp that same day. Now more inmates than ever were interested in learning about Mr. Wong's special friend.

The guards tolerated the activity again for a time, but then they decided it was time to teach him a lesson that would stop his witnessing once and for all. They had tortured him and broken his bones, but they had failed to kill him. If they couldn't kill him, maybe the elements could.

It was winter, and the temperature was incredibly cold—far below zero. They removed his clothes and tied his hands and feet to a post outdoors. Maybe he had been unconscious the first time they threw him on the dead pile. Maybe they had not actually broken his bones, and that was how he had walked back to camp unharmed. Maybe his body was naturally immune to the poisons of the Qinghai grass, for he thrived on the stuff. But the cold would kill him, they laughed to themselves. This time they were sure they would be rid of this troublesome man.

Left alone in the dark, Mr. Wong considered his options. He could freeze to death, or he could trust God and pray.

He prayed to his friend Jesus. A presence came and left. The ropes were loose! He wriggled his hands and feet out of the ropes. He was free! *An angel must have untied the ropes,* he thought.

Performing exercises helped keep him warm during the night. But as the new day began to dawn, Mr. Wong began to worry that if the guards would find him unfettered, they would blame his friends in the camp with whom he talked about Jesus. The guards might torture or even kill them.

He didn't want to cause them grief unwittingly, so he retied his ankles easily enough. But tying his wrists behind his back posed a problem. He needed an extra pair of hands! But then how would he tie up the extra pair afterward? There seemed no human solution.

So he prayed again. "Lord, You sent my guardian angel to untie me. Now, please send him back to tie me up again!"

He felt the ropes tighten around his hands, and he was held fast to the post. It was none too soon. He could hear the guard approaching.

When the guards found Mr. Wong's skin rosy pink and not pale blue, they were angry indeed. Why couldn't they kill this man who always talked about Jesus?

Grudgingly they began to untie the knots. Undoing the rope at his feet was no problem, but at his wrists the knot was so tight it took the guard a half hour to get it loose. Mr. Wong couldn't help thinking to himself that his guardian angel either didn't know his own strength or had a delightful sense of humor.

Later, back in the prison Mr. Wong became known as the man the prison guards could not kill. From that time on, the guards stopped trying to teach him a lesson and looked the other way when he talked about his friend Jesus.

The years rolled by. Chairman Mao died, and the Gang of Four gained control briefly. Then in 1979, a reform-minded Deng XiaoPing replaced the notorious Gang. Deng himself had suffered under the Cultural Revolution, and the memory was fresh on his mind. Deng wanted to free those in prison, so Mr. Wong was one of the first to be released in 1979, and later sent a letter of reinstatement. He is one of the few survivors of Qinghai. Out of 1,500 people who entered Qinghai, only 100 left alive.

Today Mr. Wong is in his 80s, but he looks like a man 20 years younger. And he has enough energy to tire a man half his age.

Many people in China think the Cultural Revolution wasted 10 years of their lives, but Mr. Wong has a special reward from his so-called lost years. He proudly shows his collection of letters from other survivors of Qinghai, saying that his experience in prison inspired them to believe his God exists. They thank him for talking about his friend Jesus. And he still talks about his friend Jesus to whomever will listen.

♦ ♦ ♦